MISS MILLINGTON'S UNEXPECTED SUITOR (ONLY FOR LOVE #6)

A CLEAN REGENCY ROMANCE

ROSE PEARSON

LANDON HILL MEDIA

MISS MILLINGTON'S
UNEXPECTED SUITOR

PROLOGUE

"*F*inally, I am to truly make my come out."

Constance twirled around the drawing room in excitement as happiness flooded through her soul. There was no one to dance with her for, at the moment, she was entirely alone - but that only encouraged her to spin merrily around the room. Having made her way to London with her parents only two days prior, she was filled with anticipation over the upcoming season and had been, to her mother's mind, much too eager to step out into society. Lord and Lady Hayman had insisted on resting for the last two days to recover from the journey, whilst Constance had done nothing but complain about the wait. After all, had she not been patient enough already?

Over the last two Seasons, while she had enjoyed time with her friends, she had been forced to do nothing other than watch as her elder sisters sought to find suitors. Now, however, it was to be her turn. Already she was imagining what it would be like to dance in the arms of a gentleman, and to have one in particular offer her attentions, and even courtship – though she would not hasten to marry. Her sisters had both been given the opportunity to take time over their decision of which gentleman they would call husband, and Constance was hopeful for the same. Yes, she was the last daughter, but surely that would not make any particular difference to her father.

"Constance, good gracious! Whatever are you doing? This is not a ballroom!" Her mother, having walked into the drawing room expecting to find her daughter reading quietly, or doing her embroidery, rather than dancing with an invisible gentleman, rushed forward as if she might need to grasp Constance's hand and lead her to a chair. "You *must* sit down at once. Your father is coming to speak with us both within the next few moments!"

At this, Constance's smile shattered and the happiness in her heart began to fade away. Her father was a rather strict and unaffectionate fellow, who seemed to care very little for his offspring, aside from making certain that their dowry was suitable and the prospective husband wealthy enough. After all, as he had explained on many an occasion, he wanted the very best of connections for his daughters, for they would always be linked to *his* name and *his* title. Constance knew, given his previous remarks to her sisters, that, while he took such connections very seriously, it was without any consideration for the feelings or emotions of his daughters. Their husbands had been carefully considered over two separate Seasons and each of them had obeyed all directives he had given them.

Silently, Constance was a little uncertain that she would be of the same ilk. She had always known her own mind, and in this matter was all the more determined.

"What does he want to speak of, Mama?"

Lady Hayman waved a hand.

"If I knew, my dear, then I would have already told

you," she stated. "You know very well that your father keeps most matters to himself. It would not be right for me to ask him when he is clearly unwilling to speak of it to me in advance of this conversation."

Constance turned her face away so that her mother would not see the roll of her eyes. She thought it most ridiculous that a gentleman would not speak to his wife about their daughter, especially when it came to the matter of marriage, but then again, her father had always been inclined towards privacy. He had always expected that his wife would simply listen to whatever he had to say and would do as he instructed - and his daughters the same. It was to his chagrin that Constance was a little less than willing to be as he expected, for she was always the one who stepped out of the bounds he set her. To her mind, she was simply free-spirited and determined, which she did not think were particularly undesirable traits, though her mother and elder sisters had tried their very best to disagree and to change her character into something they thought more appropriate.

A small, wry smile pulled at her mouth as she recalled how her sister had declared at the beginning of last Season that ladies of the *ton* ought to show nothing but respect and deference, particularly if they were eager to be married. She had laughed and thrown up her hands, questioning aloud what sort of gentleman would want a spirited young lady for a bride. Constance had listened to all of their claims and concerns but as the Season continued and she, who was not out, was forced only to watch her sisters and their friends, she had silently become aware of the many *other* young ladies who were not as quiet nor as pious as her sisters. In addition to this, she had also silently promised herself - as well as verbally agreed with her friends - that she would not marry any gentleman unless he loved her, and she loved him in return. This had not been said to her father, mother, nor to her sisters, for no doubt they would either all laugh at her, or encourage her to think otherwise. This vow to herself was the reason why now, her father's visit was bringing with it a mounting concern.

"You do know that you have been given a very significant opportunity here in London." Her mother sat quickly and gracefully, smoothing her skirts with one hand. "I was concerned that your father would not bring you here at all, but you must see, now, how considerate he has been to give you this chance."

Turning her head back to face her mother, Constance frowned.

"You did not think he would bring me to London? Even though I am to have a Season?"

Lady Hayman shook her head.

"You know as well as I that your father has always been taken up with business affairs. Of late, he has been so very busy with the improvements at the estate, which are not yet finished, that I was not sure that he would wish to leave, to come here." With a smile, she settled back in her chair as though Constance ought to understand. "I believe at one point he was considering Baron Stratton."

At the mention of this particular gentleman, Constance shuddered. Baron Stratton was a gentleman who had long lived on an estate near her father's and, over the years, he had made it quite clear that he was *more* than eager to marry one of Lord Hayman's daughters. Constance had never thought him a genuine consideration, however, believing that her father would feel much same, but it appeared now that she had been entirely mistaken.

"I was easily able to dissuade him, once I heard of the

scheme," Lady Hayman smiled as Constance sank back into her chair, suddenly rather nervous about what her father might now be coming to say. What if her mother was mistaken, and Baron Stratton was now in London? "You need not look so worried, my dear. I have assured him that such a thing would not be right. Baron Stratton would not be a suitable match."

"He certainly would not be." Shaking her head, Constance turned her attention to the window, rather than look at her mother. "Why should father think that the Baron would be suitable for me when he is almost of an age with Father himself-"

Her consideration was brought to a swift close, for the door opened and Lord Hayman entered. Constance rose, as was expected, and then sat again when her father waved one hand at her. Standing in front of the fireplace, he put his hands behind his back and then fixed sharp grey eyes upon Constance.

"Constance, of late, I have been considering your future." Constance opened her mouth to say that she had very little idea that her father had been considering anything about her, save for the fact that he would bring her to London, and the Marriage Mart. However, given the way that her father sniffed and lifted his chin, she wisely chose to keep her mouth closed. Lord Hayman continued, without even glancing at her, instead letting his gaze fix itself to the wall at the opposite end of the room as if he were talking to that rather than to his daughter. "I have not the time nor the patience to permit you to find yourself a suitable match. Therefore," he continued firmly, "I shall find a suitable match for you. You will be wed by the end of the Season."

Shock pushed itself into Constance's heart, rendering

her speechless. She stared, aghast, at her father, who managed a small smile, albeit still directed at the wall, as if to congratulate himself on doing something so considerate for her.

"Father." Managing to find her voice, Constance immediately tried to express her lack of eagerness to be given such a match. "I appreciate that you are very taken up with estate matters but surely, since you allowed my sisters to find suitable husbands for themselves, I should be treated with the same consideration."

"It is a different situation. I was not involved in estate improvements during either of your sisters' Seasons." Her father flapped one hand at her, dismissively. "I am afraid I do not have time for such things with you. I will find a suitable gentleman as quickly as I can and then we will return home so that you might prepare for the wedding." As Lord Hayman continued with his explanation about why he was required back at the estate as soon as could be and why, therefore, he could not spend any length of time in London, Constance blinked rapidly to push back her tears. To cry at this juncture would make very little difference. Most likely, if he caught her tears, her father would snort and then exit the room, leaving her to her mother's care. It was not as though her begging or pleading would make any difference, for, as she well knew, what her father decided was what happened – regardless of anyone else's opinion. That was the sort of gentleman he was, a gentleman who chose to act in any way he wished and expected no consequences for those choices. "As I have said. I will be looking for a gentleman who might be suitable. Indeed, I shall be looking from this very evening!" He rose from his chair again and made his way directly to the door. "I will inform you of his name very soon, I hope."

The door closed behind him, and Constance immediately burst into tears. Her mother rose at once, hurrying over to her, her arm going around Constance's shoulders as she murmured words of comfort. When Constance could lift her face just a little to look at her mother, it was clear that Lady Hayman was just as astonished as she, for her face had gone rather pale, and her eyes were still wide.

"I am sure that your father will pick a most suitable gentleman." Her words made very little difference to the pain in Constance's heart, for what sort of young lady truly wished to marry a gentleman simply because her father had chosen him? Yes, he might be suitable in terms of title and wealth, but she, on the other hand, would only care for his character, whether he was kind or gentle. What if her father chose a man whose character was deeply flawed, who had no interest in a wife save for what her dowry might bring him? What if he was a gentleman without heart, without consideration? She could not tie herself to a gentleman like that! Constance did not want to be married to such a man, having already determined to marry someone who loved her. But how was she to do so, now, when her father had made his decision already? "Please, do not cry." Pulling out a handkerchief, Lady Hayman handed it to Constance, who dabbed her eyes. Despite her mother's soft cajoling, she was entirely unable stop her tears from flowing. "I am sure that it will not be as difficult a situation as you might think. The gentleman you wed will be more than excellent, I assure you."

"I cannot feel the same certainty." Constance closed her eyes tightly, dampness on her cheeks, her shoulders rounding. "Mama, this is not at all what I had planned for the Season. I wanted to be given my opportunity, as my sisters were given, to find a suitable husband – a man who was of my own choosing while, at the same time, being a gentleman Father approved of. Why is my father so determined to steal this chance from me? Why am I to be treated in such a manner?"

As her mother attempted to make an explanation, Constance's eyes continued to fill with tears. It did not matter what Lady Hayman said. The truth was, her future was now very dark indeed, and it seemed that not even the smallest chink of light could be shone upon it.

CHAPTER ONE

*A*dam blinked.
      "I do not understand."

"What is there to understand?" Lady Margaret laughed and ran one finger from his shoulder all the way down to his heart. "Surely you must see that I have no desire to attach myself to any *one* gentleman. I thought I made that clear from the beginning of our acquaintance."

"No, you did not." Adam blinked rapidly, trying to take in this new situation. "I came here professing my love for you. I had every intention of..." His words trailed off as she fluttered one hand at him before going to sit down, leaving him standing by the fireplace. "Did you not realize that *this* is why your mother has departed? She is aware of my intentions."

To his utter dismay, Lady Margaret, the young lady to whom he had given his affections for so long, simply laughed again and shook her head.

"You cannot be so foolish as to think that I would possibly be in love with you." A teasing smile crossed her lips. "I do not give my heart to anyone, for that is foolishness. No, I shall marry a gentleman who has the very best of wealth and fortune and who holds the highest title. Let us see which gentleman can snare me!" Her eyes glittered, and Adam shrank back. "I only want the very best, and I am afraid that, at this point, you are *not* the very best gentleman of my acquaintance. I may, in time, decide to return to you – so do not fear that this is the end of our acquaintance."

The carelessness with which she spoke had Adam's heart burning with agony. This was not the young lady he thought himself in love with, was it? One who took his affections and laughed at them? Yes, it had only been three weeks since their first acquaintance but, since then, they had spent a good deal of time together. They had walked together, conversed together, taken tea together and they had already walked in the park on three separate occasions. He had found himself so enchanted that it had been difficult to look at anyone else. Then again, he had reasoned, why should he think about any other? If he had Lady Margaret, then he wanted no other.

Now, however, it seemed as though his consideration of the lady and his hopes for their future together had been nothing but foolishness. Lady Margaret did not love him, did not even care for him, and thus, he now knew himself to be a fool.

"As I have said," Lady Margaret murmured, sniffing and turning her head away in a somewhat dismissive manner. "If you are a gentleman willing to wait for me then I might choose to return to you. In truth, it rests upon whether or not I can garner the sole attentions of one *particular* gentleman – the Marquess of Hadenshire?" She laughed again and Adam shuddered at the sound. "I know, you will tell me that you are *also* a Marquess and, whilst that is true, I believe that the Marquess of Hadenshire has a good deal more wealth *and* property than you, although your fortune is more than suitable also, of course." Adam felt as if her words were beginning to press down upon him, pushing him lower and lower into the floor as they stole his hopes from him. "If it is that Lord Hadenshire can be persuaded to consider me, then I *am* afraid that our acquaintance would have to come to an end in its entirety."

Adam blinked, attempting to piece together everything that Lady Margaret was telling him. It was not at all what he had expected from her. It was astonishing, overwhelming, and deeply distressing, sending a pain through him that he had never anticipated for even a moment. How could she be so dismissive, so cruel? The lady he had doted upon, the lady he had dreamt of taking as his wife, had decided to pull his heart from his chest and stamp upon it with her delicate feet until there was no hope for its recovery.

"I do hope that I have not injured you in any way." With a small sigh, a brief smile, and another sigh, Lady Margaret rose from her seat and gestured to the door, stating clearly – without words - that their meeting was at an end. Her voice was measured and steely as she said, "It certainly cannot be any great affection, Lord Seaton, for it is only three weeks since our first acquaintance, and I am certain that *any* sort of affection takes a good deal longer to even *begin* to bloom. Besides," she finished, with another wave of her hand, "I am not at all inclined towards affection. I think only of practicality and my requirements. And I require the very best of gentlemen – and I hope that Lord Hadenshire will prove himself to be so."

And thus, with those words chasing him, Adam was forced to take his leave, with the sound of her voice ringing in his ears.

Just like that, he was dismissed from her presence, and

pushed away from her company. Their meeting was at an end, his discussion with her concluded. There was nothing else for him to say, nothing else which she would *permit* him to say, for even his protests that he loved her desperately and could not bear to be separated from her had brought no change. Nothing had been offered to him in response. She could only laugh and wave one hand at him, dismissing such grand feelings as being nothing more than a jest. She claimed that his feelings were not particularly strong and that she had not given him an impression of affection, while he felt very certain that she *had* done so. Why else would she have been eager for his company? Why had she accepted everything he had offered her without question? It made very little sense.

Striding from the house, he dismissed his carriage with a wave of his hand, stating aloud that he intended to walk. The coachman nodded and pulled away without another word, leaving Adam to stride forward alone. He could not abide the idea of sitting silently in his carriage with Lady Margaret's words haunting him. No, he was much too angry. He needed now to walk until his upset dissipated.

How could Lady Margaret treat him like this? His affection had been profound, his professions of love had been speaking the truth from his heart but, instead of responding in kind, she had rejected him with a laugh, as though his heart were not about to break by her dismissal. He waited for anger to lick across his skin and, though it came, something more came with it. Was it grief? Sadness? Mortification that he had been so easily deceived? Had his heart truly been so gullible?

Mayhap I was a little hasty.

Having only been to London for part of the previous Season, and none of the two Seasons before that, due to estate matters taking up all of his time, he had been delighted to fall in love so quickly. It had not originally been his intention to be gone from society for so long but, since taking on the title upon his father's passing some years ago, he had been required to work through a great many wrongs and solve complex difficulties, for his father had not dealt well with the estate in his later years. With such things now concluded, and the estate running tolerably well, he had decided that what was next required was to find himself a wife. She would have to be a young lady of excellent character, genteel, from a suitable family, and someone who would accept the affections of his heart. Last Season, he had permitted himself some joviality and the like, but had also been considering every young lady he met. This Season, however, he had settled upon Lady Margaret and, due to her interest in his company, he had soon found himself deeply drawn to her. Now, however, it appeared that any indication of affection or even interest on her part had been words only, words which, no doubt, she shared with many a gentleman, given that she had not been spending time only in *his* company.

I am a fool.

Rubbing one hand down over his face, Adam blew out a long breath in the hope that a modicum of those feelings would soon leave him but, to his frustration, they did not. Instead, the emotion lingered, her words spinning around his mind, her laughter biting into him so that his mortification and anger grew with every step he took. He had no doubt that Lady Margaret would tell others of his profession of love, for she was not a young lady inclined to keep such things to herself. This meant that, very soon, the *ton* would know of his expressions of affection and, thereafter, of her subsequent rejection. No doubt there would be many who would laugh at him, would mock him both within his hearing and out of it, for it did not matter how much pain or embarrassment he felt, the *ton* would be more than willing to add to it.

"Goodness! Do watch where you are walking, good sir!"

Adam stumbled back, stammering an apology, his thoughts shattering in every direction.

"I do apologize!"

"Gentlemen ought to be watching their steps, making sure to remove themselves from the path of others. The streets of London are not provided solely for yourself!"

"Yes, yes, of course. My humblest apologies."

There was nothing else for him to say, for yes, he *had* been at fault. He had not been watching where he was going, being lost in his thoughts and, being so distracted, had almost walked into a young lady and her mother, the latter of whom was speaking to him with such firmness that it was as if she were scolding an errant boy. Heat climbed into his face, and he dropped his gaze, somewhat disconcerted as the lady continued berating him.

"I expect gentlemen of society to behave in a manner which evidences their gentility," she continued, throwing one hand about. "You might have trodden on my daughter's toes or torn her dress, and then where would we be? You could have knocked her backward and she could have suffered an injury! We all walk upon the same street, sir, and gentlemen obstructing ladies, such as ourselves, in such a fashion is neither respectable nor considerate."

"Mama, you are a little too harsh."

At this remark, Adam allowed himself to look at the young lady in question, having given her barely more than a glance thus far. She was not looking at him but rather had dropped her gaze to the ground between them as if she could not bring herself to look into his face.

"*I* do not think so." The lady shook off her daughter's hand and her concern. "When we first set foot out of doors this afternoon, it was with the expectation that every other member of the *ton* would behave just as they ought, rather than acting with such inconsideration."

"Yes, of course." Hoping to put an end to the tirade, Adam inclined his head and spoke with firmness. "You are quite correct in everything which you have said. I was not paying even the slightest bit of attention to my steps and could very well have walked into you both. For that, I can only apologize." Lifting his head, he put out both hands. "Might I enquire if you are both quite well after our near collision?"

"There is nothing to speak of since nothing took place."

The young woman finally lifted her eyes to his and, for a moment Adam could do nothing but stare into them. The green and soft hazel shades within them were so vivid, they were so unlike the eyes of any other young lady he had met thus far that he was startled. With a small frown, he took in the redness beneath her eyes and the way that her lips turned slightly down. Was she sorrowful over some matter or other? Had something happened to make her feel so?

Dismissing the thought, for it was not his business to know or to even enquire, he quickly returned his attention to the older lady.

"I can only, once more, apologize and beg you for your forgiveness."

The young lady tutted aloud, catching both Adam and her mother's attention.

"You have no need to apologize so profusely. Nothing at all occurred!"

"Be that as it may, I will openly admit that I should have been taking more care. I was quite lost in my own thoughts and not at all considerate, as has been stated so clearly." He was not about to explain the reasons behind his strangeness of mood but, when the young lady's gaze met his, an overwhelming desire to tell her everything flared with him. Attempting to quench such an idea, he turned his head and looked away from her, breaking their connection and finding himself relieved when the sensation passed. "I will endeavor to take much more care in the future."

The older lady lifted her chin, a spark of victory in her eyes.

"That is most pleasing. Might I enquire as to your name? We are certainly not acquainted for I have an excellent memory and do not ever remember being introduced to you."

Fearing that she was going to take his name and then gossip about what had occurred to her friends and acquaintances, Adam shrugged inwardly. After all, it was not as though he could refuse to answer.

"The Marquess of Seaton, my Lady."

Clearing his throat gently, he bowed low and then straightened, seeing the lady's eyes widen just a little. Mayhap, upon hearing his title, she now viewed him with a little more consideration, and might decide *not* to gossip about him to her friends.

"A *Marquess*," she remarked, sending a pointed look towards her daughter who, much to Adam's surprise, huffed a little, rolled her eyes and turned her gaze away in a very obvious fashion. "How very pleased we are to make your acquaintance! Permit me to introduce myself and my daughter - I am Lady Hayman and this is my youngest daughter, Miss Constance Millington."

"Delighted."

Miss Millington's voice held no genuine happiness and whilst she curtsied and said the correct things, Adam could not help but wonder at the way Miss Millington had rolled her eyes. Was it that she found this new connection to be of very little interest? Or perhaps it was that her mother's obvious eagerness had frustrated her a little - but even that in itself was surprising. Surely every young lady in London had the intention to acquaint themselves with as many highly titled gentlemen as they could, in the hope of snaring one of them. Why, then, would she be so obviously disinterested?

"I do hope I will have the pleasure of standing up with you very soon." He spoke before even the thought had come to mind. "It would be a pleasure to dance with you, Miss Millington, I am sure, and perhaps, might allow me to make up for my lack of consideration this afternoon."

"You need have no need to concern yourself in that regard," she answered quickly, only for her mother to laugh loudly and grasp her daughter's hand.

"What my daughter means to say is that yes, she would be *more* than delighted, Lord Seaton."

When the mother quickly covered her daughter's first answer with one of her own. Miss Millington remained silent, her gaze now pulling away from her mother, away from Adam, and towards the other side of the street, indicating, he assumed, a complete lack of interest in any further conversation.

Adam was not at all insulted, however. Instead, he simply found a sense of curiosity that began to twist around his heart. This young lady was quite remarkable, given that she was so obvious in her expressions. Why any young lady would not wish to stand up with a gentleman such as himself, with his title, was quite beyond him and, despite the awareness that they had only just met, Adam was eager to discover the answer.

"I must take my leave of you both, and again, I beg your pardon for my lack of consideration." He inclined his head again. "There is much I must do before the evening arrives."

"Oh, and what occasion are you to attend this evening?"

With a small smile. Adam spoke to Lady Hayward but continued to glance at Miss Millington, who was still looking away from him.

"I am bound to Lord Buckston's soiree," he answered, only for Lady Hayward's face to light up with obvious delight, whereas her daughter remained entirely stoic.

"I am delighted to hear it," she said with a broad smile. "We shall be in attendance also, with my husband, Viscount Hayward. I *do* hope that it will be an excellent evening and mayhap, we might have the pleasure of talking with you again."

Adam nodded, smiled, and stepped away. The moment he was gone from Miss Millington and her mother's company, however, the thoughts of Lady Margaret returned, and his spirits once more fell low.

He had declared himself, and she had done nothing but laugh at his profession of love. Questions began to nag at him and, as he strode in the direction of his townhouse, Adam's jaw set tight.

Had her mockery been deserved?

Was what he felt truly a heart filled with love, or was he nothing more than a fool for ever believing that such an emotion could be real?

CHAPTER TWO

*C*onstance sighed heavily as her friend's smile fell.

"It is of great sorrow to me, of course. I am to be led to my future by my father, whether I wish it or not."

"Do not permit yourself to be so troubled," her friend reassured her warmly. "Many a father has said such a thing, I am sure, but they do not always follow through on such statements."

"Alas, you do not know my father." A stone dropped into her stomach and her lips twisted for a moment. "He is the most stubborn of gentlemen with very little consideration for others." Shooting a look to Lady Winterbrook, she sighed and threw her head back, her eyes squeezing closed as she groaned aloud. "Now, do not look at me with such an aghast expression on your face. I am speaking honestly, as I have every right to do, given that he is my father and you my most trustworthy friend."

Lady Winterbrook hesitated, then nodded, although she looked away.

"I suppose I can give you that," she admitted, after some moments. "It must be very distressing indeed to be told that your hopes for the future have been entirely dashed, simply because your father desires to get back to his estate quickly."

"It is all the more distressing to know that I am not worthy of his time."

With a heavy heart, Constance looked away, a little surprised to find that she was close to tears, again, about her father's dismissal, which had hurt her so severely.

"I can see that." Lady Winterbrook squeezed her hand reassuringly. "But there must be something we can do. Some of your friends are here together for the Season, aside from Lady Sherbourne, given she is due to enter her confinement soon. But those of us who are here in London can certainly be of aid to you."

Constance turned her head and looked directly into Lady Winterbrook's face.

"Are you quite certain?" she asked softly. "I know that we made a promise to each other, but since you are now all wed, I would understand if your desire to be of aid to me is a little lessened." Her face grew hot as she spoke. "I am all too aware that I am the last to make my come out, forced into waiting to do so until my elder sisters were finally wed. I had thought that my father might give me last Season along with Judith, but no, I had to wait until she was married before I could make my come out, albeit a little later than the rest of you."

For the last two Seasons, Constance had been with her friends and enjoyed their company, while at the same time, she had not been permitted to dance as freely as they, nor to even consider courtship or the like. Instead, she had stayed a little further back as a wallflower might, forced to wait until her father stated that she might have *her* Season. It seemed cruel now to deprive her of her freedom and insist that she marry a gentleman of his choosing rather than allowing her to make her own choice.

"My dear Constance, you need not have any such fears." With a warm smile, Lady Winterbrook encouraged her quietly. "From the very beginning, we promised one another that we would support each other in our endeavors to marry for love, rather than for practicality's sake. Simply because we are all wed and settled does not mean we have forgotten you."

This was spoken with a slight flickering frown passing across Lady Winterbrook's forehead, and Constance closed her eyes, a little ashamed.

"Forgive me, I ought not to have questioned your loyalty."

"And there is no shame in being the last of us," Lady Winterbrook told her firmly. "None of us think less of you. We understand your situation, and are glad to be of aid to you, in whatever way we can be."

With a small sigh, Constance put out her hands, then let them drop them back to her sides.

"Mayhap the only thing I require from all of you is your support to help me accept my situation. I shall not have the chance to marry for love, as you have all done. My father has decided and that is the end of it."

Lady Winterbrook tipped her head.

"Unless...?"

With a frown, Constance looked at her friend, catching the gentle glimmer in her eyes. Had she already hit upon an idea? Constance would take anything if it meant giving herself the same opportunity as her sisters.

"You say that your father has not yet found a suitable gentleman for you?"

Wordlessly, Constance nodded, having very little idea of what her friend was thinking.

"Then it is very simple!" Lady Winterbrook chuckled. "You must find a gentleman to fall in love with, and when he falls in love with you also, you will present him to your father as the most suitable of all gentlemen in London."

Her shoulders dropped as Constance attempted to smile, but shook her head at the same time.

"Whilst I appreciate the idea, I do not think it will be as easy as that. As I have said, my father is eager to choose my husband for me, and he will do so quickly."

"Then you must simply fall in love quickly," Lady Winterbrook stated as if such a thing was perfectly straightforward. "And the gentleman must fall in love with you too, although I do not think that will take any great length of time."

A flush touched Constance's cheeks at the compliment.

"You are very kind."

"I am quite serious!" Lady Winterbrook exclaimed, grasping her hand again. "You are quite lovely, you know, and I am sure that many a gentleman will be eager to make your acquaintance and, thereafter, to fall quite in love with you."

Constance smiled gently.

"And while that is kind, it does not offer me any particular solution, though I am grateful to you for your suggestion."

"Then why do you not use 'The London Ledger'?"

At this, Constance frowned.

"How could I use 'The London Ledger' to my advantage?"

Thinking of the publication that Lady Yardley prepared and then published for society's enjoyment during the

London Season, Constance waited for Lady Winterbrook to explain her idea a little more. It took some moments – for Lady Winterbrook was clearly thinking it through before she spoke.

"It could be used to search for a gentleman who might be as eager to make a match of love and affection, such as you are." Lady Winterbrook lifted both shoulders as Constance's frown grew. "It is difficult to ascertain such things through only introduction and acquaintance, of course, but to do it this way will make things a good deal easier for you, I am sure. For if a gentleman is unwilling to allow his heart to feel such things – though such things, very often, can capture him regardless – then would it not be best to know of it in advance of furthering your acquaintance? Therefore, you could concentrate your efforts on those who might respond with positive interest in a match of love." She smiled as Constance bit her lip. "It is certainly not the most conventional method to seek out a husband, and I will admit that it may cause some difficulties, but given that you have restricted time, perhaps this would not be so unwise a consideration."

Constance shook her head.

"I do not think that such a thing would work," she stated plainly, only to see her friend's crestfallen expression. She quickly forced a smile. "I shall consider it, however."

With a smile that did not quite touch every part of her eyes, Lady Winterbrook nodded.

"That is something, at least," she said softly. "Come now, we should not stand alone in this corner conversing for too long. I am sure my husband will be in search of me soon and I am sure that Lady Yardley would like to speak with you also. Have you spoken with her yet this Season?"

"No, not as yet."

Her heart filled with a sudden hope, for speaking to Lady Yardley was certain to calm her fears a little. The lady was very calm and considered, and would perhaps offer her some other advice, save from using 'The London Ledger'.

"Then come, let me take you to her."

They walked together only a few steps, beginning to cross the room, only for a gentleman to come to stand in front of them, stopping them both.

"Good evening."

He was looking at Constance with an expression and a smile that suggested she was already acquainted with him, but as Constance searched her mind, she could not recall his name, nor why they might have been already acquainted.

"Good evening."

She forced a quick smile then dropped a curtsey, glancing at Lady Winterbrook in the hope that her friend might already be aware of this fellow. To her dismay, Lady Winterbrook's expression did not inspire any sort of confidence in that regard.

"And how are you this evening?"

His smile grew a little wider, with a softness about his eyes, and Constance found herself looking back into his face, her thoughts becoming a little more panicked as she fought to recall him.

"I am well, I thank you."

The gentleman chuckled softly, tilting his head to one side.

"And none the worse for our *almost* altercation?"

He asked the question with a grin, as she suddenly remembered exactly who he was and how they had been acquainted. Relief pooled in her stomach, and she relaxed her shoulders, glad now to recognize his face.

"No, indeed, none whatsoever, especially given that there was no altercation to speak of!"

Laughing, he looked to Lady Winterbrook and fresh panic wound its way through Constance's veins. No doubt he would soon ask or expect to be introduced to Lady Winterbrook, and try as she might, while she could remember him speaking his title, she couldn't recall a word of what he had said. Yes, they had spoken on the street together, but she had been so distracted by what her father had told her, she had not paid great attention to what had been said and had deliberately rolled her eyes at her mother when she had made some remark about him.

He has a high title, I am sure.

Her brow furrowed. Why had she not paid more attention? She had been deeply frustrated with her mother for making such a scene when there had been very little to become upset about in the first place, then he had apologized and, after some more complaints from her mother, she had then asked for his title.

What was it?

"I must beg you to introduce me to your friend."

Realizing that there had been a beat or two of silence, Constance cleared her throat.

"Yes, of course."

The gentleman smiled in the direction of Lady Winterbrook, who then threw a glance at Constance, only to widen her eyes a little, evidently aware of Constance's inability to do what had been asked of her. Constance took in a breath, forced a smile, and searched desperately for what she might say.

"Perhaps I may be mistaken, but I am sure that we are already acquainted." Clearly seeking to assist Constance, Lady Winterbrook quickly spoke up so that Constance would not feel any sort of embarrassment. "It may have been when I was unmarried, however? I was Lady Elizabeth, but I am now Lady Winterbrook."

The gentleman cleared his throat, then inclined his head a little.

"Forgive me, I do not recall it, although if we have already been introduced, I apologize for my forgetfulness. I am the Marquess of Seaton."

When he bowed low, Constance quickly closed her eyes in relief before opening them again and putting a warm smile on her face.

"I am very glad to make your acquaintance... again."

With a quiet laugh, Lady Winterbrook curtsied, then looked quickly towards Constance, her eyebrows lifting gently. Constance simply ignored the look, however, knowing full well what it meant. Yes, he was a Marquess, but that meant very little to her. Of course, his title was one her father would accept, but all the same, she would not simply tie herself to him because of his title or standing.

"Miss Millington, since there is to be no dancing this evening, might I hope that I can secure your dance card for the next ball, provided you are to be in attendance?"

Constance smiled quickly.

"But of course." It would not be right of her to refuse a gentleman's request and, secretly, she was glad that someone was willing to dance with her already. It would mean that she would not be standing back, hoping that her dance card would fill. "I am to attend Lord Hanley's ball tomorrow evening."

Lord Seaton smiled.

"Capital. I am to be in attendance also, so that will suit us both very well, and I shall be able to keep the promise I made to you upon our first meeting."

Lady Winterbrook asked him something about how long he had been in London and while the gentleman answered, Constance considered his features. Hair that fell carelessly across his forehead, sharp eyes which seemed to take everything in at once, but were certainly warm in their considerations.

He was, she thought, someone who many would consider to be fairly handsome, and, given that he was a Marquess, he would be seen as all the more so, surely? This thought then led her to wonder why he was not betrothed or married already, given his high title. Surely marriage was a requirement since he would need an heir to that title? Mayhap, she considered, tilting her head a little, he had, perhaps, a desire to remain without the attachment of a wife for a time, as so many other gentlemen appeared to want. They sought out pleasure and excitement rather than any sort of genuine commitment. She had seen such gentlemen during her time in London, while her sisters were seeking matches. Mayhap the Marquess was such a fellow.

With a shake of her head, she looked away, aware that she was judging him much too harshly, and based solely on appearance alone. For all she knew, he might be an excellent sort, who as yet, had not found the right young lady to take as his bride.

"You appear to be considering something most deeply, Miss Millington."

It was as if a fire had been set by her feet, such was the heat of her embarrassment. She had been so lost in her own contemplations that she had not been aware that Lord Seaton had been doing much the same, clearly wondering what it was that she was thinking of during her study of him.

"I was merely considering my recent conversation with

you and wishing that we had been introduced under better circumstances." It was a terrible lie, of course, but she could not exactly tell him that she had been wondering why he was not wed, as yet. "It was deeply embarrassing, for my esteemed mother was much too overwrought - and for that, I am profoundly sorry."

The gentleman merely laughed and clasped both hands behind his back.

"Pray, do not let it concern you any longer. After all, I was the one who walked into you... or nearly did, at least."

"All the same, I do hope that you were not too discomfited."

His smile stole away any further concern.

"I was made aware of my foolishness, and rightly so. Therefore, I shall now make certain to always have my head lifted and my gaze fixed upon the path ahead of me, so that I might know where I am going, and who I might inadvertently walk into if I am not careful."

Chuckling at this, he smiled broadly, and Constance found herself smiling back at him. He was a very considerate gentleman, she thought, easily amenable to all and every situation.

"I am relieved to hear it, Lord Seaton."

"But of course." Inclining his head, he took a step back. "Now, I shall leave you both, for I am sure that there will be many eager to converse with you, and I do not want to claim too much of your time." His eyes went back to Constance. "And do remember that I am to claim your first dance at Lord Hanley's ball." he reminded her as she smiled. "Do not forget me!"

She laughed, promised him that she would remember and, as he walked away, she allowed her gaze to settle on him, watching as he made his way across the room.

"The Marquess of Seaton." Lady Winterbrook glanced in Constance's direction. "A most amiable gentleman, I think."

"Yes, I quite agree," Constance stated without hesitation. "However, I am ashamed to say that I could not remember his name, and confess how grateful I am to you for your aid."

"But of course." Lady Winterbrook laughed and put her arm through Constance's. "However, I am certain that you will not forget anything about him now. Not now that you have been in his company, seen his smile, and recalled his title."

Constance opened her mouth to say that she had no intention of forgetting the gentleman's title, for one embarrassment was *more* than enough, only to realize what her friend meant. With a slightly choked laugh, she looked away so that her eyes were no longer lingering on Lord Seaton.

"You think I ought to consider Lord Seaton?"

"Why should you not?" Lady Winterbrook smiled, leading her across the room in search of Lady Yardley. "Perhaps it may be that this meeting will lead to something quite remarkable, just as you desire."

With a sigh, Constance shook her head, dismissing Lady Winterbrook's remarks, thinking of them as nothing more than a jest. The chances of such a thing happening were so very small, to her mind, that she did not consider it even a remote possibility. With this, she cast Lord Seaton from her mind and turned her thoughts to Lady Yardley instead.

CHAPTER THREE

*T*here was a loud exclamation, but Adam paid very little attention. He had been enjoying the evening thus far and such chatter was to be expected at a social occasion such as this. It had been a few days now since he had been told by Lady Margaret that his love was nothing more than a jest and, since then, he had done his utmost to make sure that every thought of her was pushed aside almost as quickly as it came. To his surprise – and his relief – it had not been as difficult as he'd anticipated. Mayhap, he considered, now that he knew of her true character, it was easier to dismiss the feelings which had bound him to her.

And because new acquaintances have brought my heart a little levity.

He smiled as he thought of Miss Millington, only to chase that thought away and pull his smile straight. He was not going to allow his heart to be caught up all over again so quickly. No doubt that would only lead to yet more pain.

"You are not dancing this evening? I do not think that I

have seen you stand up once with a young lady, even though there are many standing along the sides of the ballroom."

Adam shook his head as his friend came towards him.

"Good evening, Lord Dennington." His shoulders lifted. "No, I am not to dance this evening. I am quite contented as I am."

Lord Dennington's lips twisted.

"You are not about to state that it is because you are pining for Lady Margaret, are you?"

Adam only laughed.

"You know me very well and thus, I can see why you might think I was doing so," he admitted quietly. "No, I am not as melancholy as I have been of late. I choose to stay back, to allow myself to observe rather than engage with people, simply because I wish to." A small shrug lifted his shoulders. "At times, the hubbub can be a little overwhelming, especially when I have so many thoughts and considerations within me at present." A slight frown caught his forehead as he looked around. The atmosphere in the ballroom had changed and there were some shrieks and exclamations of excitement which were a little out of the ordinary. He looked back towards Lord Dennington. "As you can see here for yourself!"

Lord Dennington chuckled ruefully.

"There is always some sort of gossip or rumor flying around, is there not?"

Adam sighed heavily.

"I do not doubt that whatever *this* is," he gestured to his left, to where a small group of ladies were clustered around one in particular, with another breaking away from the group to scurry across the room – no doubt to whisper into the ear of someone else. "Whatever it is, it will soon fly away, and then something more will follow it.

"Just so long as these whispers are not about either of us, we can safely ignore them."

Lord Dennington laughed as Adam grinned.

"I can easily admit that I have done nothing worthy of gossip."

His grin was immediately wiped from his face as he recalled *precisely* what he had done which might cause gossip to fly around about him... should Lady Margaret decide to tell the *ton* about what he had done in expressing his love for her. He could only pray that she would not. Thus far, he had been quite safe, but that could change at any moment.

"Whatever it is, it has certainly caused a stir." Frowning, Lord Dennington came to stand closer to Adam, his eyebrows lifting as the noise in the ballroom rose a little more. "Something momentous must have taken place." Swinging around towards Adam, he shrugged. "I confess that, while I am not usually enamored of gossip, I am now eager to discover what this is all about." Adam wanted to state that he had no interest whatsoever, but the words died on his lips. He could not speak such an untruth. Whilst he was unwilling to admit to as much aloud, inwardly he knew that he was just as eager as his friend. "I think I shall go and discover what is being said." Lord Dennington grinned as Adam smiled at him. "Should you like to join me? Or shall I come back and tell you once I have learned all about it?"

"I should not like you to tire yourself by having to repeat all you have learned." Seeing Lord Dennington's grin, he laughed and shook his head. "I can see that there is no use in pretending that I have no interest. There is something which has taken place and yes, I am now eager to know of it. Who shall we ask?"

"Why do we not go to these young ladies here?" Lord

Dennington gestured to a small group of young ladies and as they made their way forward, Lord Dennington opened his arms wide and smiled warmly. "My dear ladies, mayhap you might be of aid to us. We were in very pleasant conversation, only to see you all begin to speak and whisper together. I believe that you speak of me, but my friend believes you speak of him!" With a wink, he smiled at each young lady before glancing at Adam, who only grinned. "We would very much like to know who it is that you all speak of."

Lord Dennington's easy manner had the young ladies giggling and glancing at each other until one was bold enough to answer his question.

"Alas, we do not speak of either of you, but of momentous news!" Such was her excitement, the young lady grasped Lord Dennington's arm. "Are you acquainted with Lady Margaret?"

At this, the smile immediately fell from Adam's face, his laughter turning to dust in his mouth. Surely it could not be!

"Yes, I am acquainted with Lady Margaret." Lord Dennington threw Adam a quick look before turning his attention back to the lady. "What is it about her?"

"It is the most marvelous news!" she exclaimed, her eyes bright with excitement. "Only this very evening, she received a proposal from a gentleman of high title, a Marquess, and it is believed that she has accepted him!" For a moment Adam thought that this Marquess they spoke of was none other than himself, and caught himself glancing across the room as if Lady Margaret was suddenly going to come rushing towards him, declaring that she was deeply sorrowful over what she had said, how much she regretted sending him away and how she was deeply pained over their separation... and then his heart collapsed. "It is the Marquess of Hadenshire!" The young lady exclaimed aloud again, clapping her hands together. "I am sure that there will be a magnificent wedding. I do hope that I receive an invitation!"

The other young ladies said the same and continued in this manner for some minutes, but Adam heard none of what they said. He did not smile, did not look with delight upon the ladies as they spoke. Instead, he simply found himself lost in a cloud of emotions, taking in a shuddering breath just as Lord Dennington turned to him with a frown.

Flames were slowly rising within Adam, heat burning his face. Thankfully, so many of the young ladies were taken up with the news that very few of them paid the least bit of attention to his reaction, although from Lord Dennington's look of concern, he was aware it would not be a positive one. It was as if he had swallowed a snake which now curled and writhed within him. He was breathing harshly, emotions twisting up hard within him, but it was not as though he found himself broken-hearted over the fact that Lady Margaret was now betrothed. Instead, there was both anger and embarrassment. Anger that he had ever let himself be so foolish as to believe himself in love with Lady Margaret, and embarrassment now that not only was she betrothed, but she was betrothed to the very gentleman she had compared him to as well!

"Come." Lord Dennington took his arm and Adam went with him without hesitation, striding across the ballroom until they had found a quieter place where they might talk. Adam closed his eyes and sighed heavily. "Are you quite all right?"

Lord Dennington eyed Adam carefully only for Adam to sigh again.

"Yes, I am. I am a little frustrated but that, I suppose, is to be expected." Adam managed a wry laugh, but his friend only narrowed his eyes, clearly disbelieving him. "In truth, my heart does not ache nor cry over the news. Her betrothal in itself does not concern me. It is only the speed of it that has brought me some embarrassment."

"I do not think you need to feel so." Lord Dennington, who was a little relieved, given the way he smiled briefly and then pushed one hand through his hair, excused himself for a moment only to return with two glasses of brandy. "It is not as though you are the one at fault. Lady Margaret has chosen to betrothe herself to a particular sort of gentleman, but whether or not she will be happy, it is hard to say. You know that he does not truly care for her, and she does not truly care for him, but if that will satisfy them, then what else can be said?"

"I do not care about their happiness." With a small sip of his brandy, Adam continued. "It is only that I find myself frustrated at how quickly she pushed me aside, only to accept another gentleman who holds precisely the same title as I." Recalling exactly what Lady Margaret had said to him, a scowl pulled at his expression. "It is that this other fellow has more coin than I." He sniffed. "Which is a very sorrowful reason to pick a husband, I am sure."

With a grimace, Lord Dennington gestured across the room to where Lady Margaret herself had just walked in, but Adam turned his gaze away.

"Do you think that you would have been contented with a young lady such as Lady Margaret?" Lord Dennington asked. "You declared your affections for her, but what if she had not declared the same for you yet had remained willing to wed you? Would you have found yourself contented to be in her company? Would you have been glad to take her to the altar, knowing that your affections were a good deal more than her own?"

It was not something that Adam could immediately answer, and when his friend looked at him with a lifted eyebrow, he simply shrugged. The truth was, such a situation was not something he had considered before, but now that Lord Dennington had suggested it, he was questioning the happiness which he would have enjoyed had such a future come to pass.

"I believe I see what you mean," he began slowly. "You are suggesting that I ought to be relieved that I did not end up securing Lady Margaret's hand."

"Precisely." Lord Dennington shrugged. "To my mind, any young lady who behaves in the way that she did is not worthy of the affection and care offered by another." He shook his head, and his jaw grew tight for a moment. "If two people want a practical match, then they should find each other. And if two people seek a marriage of affection and the like, then they equally ought to seek out a person whose desires match their own."

A little surprised at his friend's fervency, Adam looked at him with a steady gaze.

"And which do you seek?"

Lord Dennington chuckled.

"For myself, I am not convinced either way. Therefore, I shall remain quite disinclined towards matrimony for the moment, I think."

Adam let out a small, dry laugh and, looking across the room, found his gaze settling on none other than Miss Millington. Immediately, it was as if he could breathe with ease again. Out of everyone in the room, she stood out to him, for she was not whispering or giggling. She did not have one hand clasped to her mouth, was not leaning in conspiratorially to hear whatever was being said. Instead, she simply talked quietly with a friend, smiling and nodding, but showing no excitement at what was being said by others. She did not make her way to another group of ladies, eager to find out what had occurred, as he had done, but instead seemed perfectly contented in her own conversation.

His heart lifted in great admiration. Miss Millington was, it seemed, very different from other young ladies, and he considered that to be to her advantage.

"I am glad to be free of Lady Margaret," he said aloud, his gaze still lingering on Miss Millington. "You are right. I should be – and am - relieved."

"I am delighted to hear it." Lord Dennington slapped Adam's shoulder, hard. "That is precisely the attitude which is required. You must not think too poorly of yourself, but instead see what you have been saved from. In time, that will give you the greatest relief, I am sure."

"You are right, I am certain." With a small swig of his brandy, Adam grinned back at his friend. "And despite your excellent advice, I beg of you to excuse me."

"Why?" Lord Dennington's eyes flared. "Are you leaving the ball already?"

"No, indeed I am not!" Adam scowled, looking around the ballroom. "I shall not be pushed away by this. Instead, I intend to greet someone else, that is all. Someone who will not be so eager to gossip as the rest."

He did not wait for Lord Dennington to question who this particular person might be but, instead, simply stepped away, knowing full well that Lord Dennington's gaze would follow him regardless. Coming towards Miss Millington, Adam's smile lifted high when she offered him a welcoming one of her own. She granted a sweetness to an otherwise bitter circumstance and, as Adam fell into easy conversation with her, all thought of Lady Margaret and her new betrothal fled from his mind.

He hoped that he would never permit himself to think of her again.

CHAPTER FOUR

*C*onstance spread out her hands.

"And this is the circumstance I now find myself in." Tears were behind her eyes, and she held them back carefully, not wishing to begin to weep in front of her friends. It was not as though she were ashamed of her tears, only that she wanted to speak as openly and as freely as she could, without breaking into sobs. "Even though I have been waiting for two Seasons to have my father permit me the same freedoms as my elder sisters, it appears that he is quite determined to do the opposite. He does not care about whether or not *I* am pleased with the situation, he only thinks of himself, and his specific requirements about my future husband.

"I am sorry." Lady Yardley's voice was soft with sympathy. "As I am sure the rest of your friends are also."

"Of course we are." Lady Landon nodded eagerly, her eyes wide and filled with something that looked like sorrow. "To find yourself in such a situation, after you have been waiting for so long, must be very difficult to accept."

"Though I have said that she need not accept it." Lady

Winterbrook's remark had everyone looking at her and, whilst a faint hint of red came into her cheeks, she continued without hesitating. "I am aware that Miss Millington is eager to use 'The London Ledger' for one particular purpose, but I have suggested another which I hope you do not mind if I share?"

She looked towards Constance who, after a moment, shrugged and smiled. Lady Yardley, however, was the first to speak.

"You already had something you wished to put into 'The London Ledger'?"

"Yes, I did." She threw a quick smile toward Lady Winterbrook. "It is not that I did not appreciate Lady Winterbrook's suggestion, it was only that I was not entirely convinced of it. Therefore, my idea was that, when my father tells me which gentlemen it is he is considering, I might use 'The London Ledger' to make certain that he is not a rogue? I know that you do not often put gossip in the Ledger, but mayhap a small remark about the gentleman, whoever he may be, might bring some reactions and that could tell me more of his character and his reputation. Would that suffice?"

"I am certain that it is something we could do," Lady Yardley confirmed. "But Lady Winterbrook, what were your thoughts?"

Briefly, Lady Winterbrook spoke of her idea, telling them the same thing she had told Constance herself only a few days earlier. She explained that it could be an opportunity to find a gentleman who could easily fall in love with Constance, for they were already eager to seek out a marriage where love and affection grew strong, whereas it could be very difficult to tell if a gentleman delighted in the thought or rejected it entirely, given only a brief acquaintance.

"An interesting suggestion." Lady Yardley looked towards Constance again, her eyes a little thoughtful. "And you do not warm to it, Constance?"

Feeling a little uncertain of herself, and then wondering if she appeared so very obvious in her response, Constance put one hand towards Lady Winterbrook.

"It is not that I reject Lady Winterbrook's suggestion," she said quickly. "I only feared that it might be a little... impractical. And, if I am truthful, I fear that either many gentlemen will reply, and I shall need to ascertain their truthfulness, or that none will respond at all!"

"I understand your fears." Lady Yardley considered for a moment then sighed. "Yes, there is something of a risk involved, but I would consider it a worthwhile risk. After all, it is always a mystery as to which gentlemen seek matches of suitability and convenience, and which ones seek out the hope of love as you do yourself. Some, of course, are very bold about such things, stating quite clearly what they expect, whereas others hide their thoughts away. If you were to take on Lady Winterbrook's suggestion, then any gentleman who responded to you would already be open to a marriage of love. That is what you are searching for, is it not?"

Constance blinked slowly, then nodded. Yes, she had to admit, it was exactly what she was looking for but, at the same time, it felt very odd indeed to be thinking about using 'The London Ledger' to search for such a thing. She had always thought it might be a fairly simple thing to discover, to find herself with a gentleman who could capture her heart as she might capture his. How often had she dreamt that one evening, they might look across the room at each other and somehow know that this was what was meant to be. Now, however, as she dropped her gaze to her lap, she realized that such an idea was foolish. It could not be as she hoped. Her father was determined to have her married off and married off very soon if he could find a suitable fellow. Therefore, she ought to be taking on every suggestion she could, ought she not?

"What precisely would I say?"

A few murmurs came as some of her friends talked over one idea and then another, but it was Lady Brookmire who finally offered a suitable suggestion.

"Why do you not write a letter to the gentlemen of London?" she began, the others falling silent as they listened to her. "You could write it anonymously, and it would only be ourselves who would know that you are the author. Write from your heart, tell the gentlemen of London that you seek a love match, and desire to find a gentleman who seeks the same thing. Therefore, if they find themselves so inclined, they could respond to Lady Yardley, so you might be aware of their name and their title. Thereafter, you would not have to go up to each individual and state that you recognize their name from 'The London Ledger'. It could be an accidental meeting, arranged, of course, by those of us who know of your intentions, but to the gentleman involved it would appear as though it is simply a new acquaintance."

A sudden thrill of excitement ran up Constance's spine.

"Do you really think such a thing would work?"

"I believe that it could work." Lady Yardley smiled. "And I should be glad to look through your responses, making certain that any with a *particular* reputation is thrown aside."

Wincing a little, Constance nodded slowly.

"So I should write a letter stating that I seek a marriage where I might love my husband, and where he would love me in return," she repeated, seeing her friends nod, a smile on every face. "Any gentleman who wishes for such a match also should write to Lady Yardley, so that I might be made aware of them. After that, even though they will not know of it, I will acquaint myself with each of them in turn and see if there is any connection that might be built between us. Is that all correct?"

"That is it, precisely." Lady Brookmire grinned as Lady Winterbrook clapped her hands in obvious delight. "And in addition, you can make certain that these gentlemen - for I am sure that there will be many - will be suitable enough for your father also. This is a very precise way to narrow down the number of gentlemen in London who will not only suit you, but also suit your father. I am certain that you will find a love match just as we all have."

Much to her surprise, tears grew rapidly in her eyes and Constance could not help but let one fall to her cheek. Immediately there were murmurs of concern replacing the smiles, but Constance quickly waved one hand.

"I am not upset nor sorrowful. I am only grateful. Grateful that I have friends such as yourselves, glad that I have found hope where I did not think I had any. You cannot know how much your friendship means to me. I am indebted to each and every one of you. I am overjoyed that our vow to each other has not been forgotten and that the pact we made still holds fast. I am very grateful to be able to call all of you my friends."

At this, there came words of affection and kindness given in response, but after a few moments, Lady Yardley reached across and pressed Constance's hand with her own.

"Might I suggest that there is no need to linger in

conversation with us, Miss Millington?" Seeing Constance's slight frown, she smiled warmly. "I do not mean to dismiss you, only to suggest that it would be wise to write your letter expeditiously, for I am due to publish 'The London Ledger' very soon - tomorrow in fact - and must have everything prepared for it, tonight. Would it be possible for you to write this letter before you take your leave?" All at once, a flurry of nervousness whirled up within her, as if she had quite forgotten how to put pen to paper. "Just speak from your heart," Lady Yardley added, as if she knew precisely how Constance was feeling. "Take care and consideration with what you write, certainly, but do be sure that your every word comes from within. State your desire clearly, and I am certain that you will receive many a response in return."

Feeling a little dizzy, Constance rose to her feet.

"Thank you, Lady Yardley." She looked around the room. "Thank you all. I go to write my letter this very moment."

"And we shall all find ourselves back here in a few days' time," Lady Winterbrook remarked with a smile. "And we shall be drowning under the sheer number of letters you have received in return."

With a laugh, Constance made her way to the door, her heart lifting with fresh hope. Perhaps she would be able to find a love match after all.

CHAPTER FIVE

"And are you still moping?"

Adam picked up his whisky and threw it back before slamming the glass back down on the table.

"No, not in the least."

His two friends looked at each other and chuckled.

"I hardly think such an action is evidence of happiness," Lord Dennington stated as Lord Campbell nodded sagely, before speaking.

"Come now. It has been some weeks since she has spoken of her heart-"

"Or her lack of affection within it," Lord Dennington added with a wolfish grin.

Lord Campbell threw him a roll of his eyes before continuing.

"As I have said, it has been some time weeks since you first declared yourself and discovered she was not at all inclined towards you. Surely, therefore, you must have a lessening of those feelings, particularly now."

"Why?" Adam shot back, his tone a little harsh. "Have *you* found your feelings for Miss Barrett lessening?"

At this, Lord Campbell's face fell. White stole the color from his face, and he cleared his throat, his brows falling low.

"Yes. I have. I have *no* feelings for the lady."

Guilt burned up Adam's throat and he looked away, suddenly ashamed of himself for bringing to mind the young lady whom Lord Campbell had professed to love the previous Season, only for her to step away from him.

"If you are inquiring as to whether or not I am in love with Lady Margaret, then you may be assured that I am not." Adam shook his head, recalling how quickly Lady Margaret had been able to dismiss him. "In fact, I have no affection for her in the least."

"But a great deal of hurt still lingers. I think." Lord Dennington spoke quietly, no longer jesting, but now rather serious. "The news from this evening has pained you. I thought you might have been happy, in a way."

"And precisely why should I be happy?" Adam threw back, a little more quickly than he had meant to. The shame which had burned only a few moments ago became a great and heavy torrent and he dropped his gaze. "Forgive me. I am aware that my mood is rather dark this evening. It is only because something more has occurred."

Lord Campbell frowned, clearly unaware of the situation, whilst Lord Dennington waggled one finger.

"Something more than Lady Margaret's betrothal? Or is this not at all related to the lady?"

"It is to do with Lady Margaret."

"But if you have no affection for her, why do you appear so irritated?" Lord Campbell waved one hand to garner the attention of a footman, requesting him to bring them some more brandy before turning back to Adam. "You do not care for Lady Margaret any longer – or so you have said, so why should you be so upset at her betrothal? Or is it that your heart is truly broken and your affection more genuine than you permit yourself to believe?"

The question was asked without malice and Adam took a moment to consider his reply. He had behaved harshly towards Lord Campbell once already, and did not want to do so again.

"I believe that my affection was genuine, but it was not really love," he stated, his jaw tight as he struggled to contain the ire rising within him. "I was a fool to think it – but to be treated so, with such inconsideration, when I had declared to Lady Margaret the depths of my heart, was more mortifying than I can express. And what is worse is that all of the *ton* will know of it."

Both of his friends frowned, a look of confusion fixing themselves to their faces.

"What do you mean?" Lord Campbell was the first to speak. "You cannot be suggesting that either I or Lord Dennington have said anything to anyone?"

"No, of course not." Accepting the glass of brandy from the footman, he shook his head, but stared down at the table, his hand gripping the glass tightly. "Lady Margaret's mother, the indomitable Lady Farlinger, has decided to declare to all and sundry that this was not the first proposal her daughter had received."

Lord Dennington snatched in a breath as Lord Campbell closed his eyes tightly.

"Precisely."

Gritting his teeth, Adam dropped his head, a low groan escaping him.

"I take it that she also saw fit to declare that *you* were the gentleman who had previously proposed?"

With a nod, Adam dropped his head all the more, his chin to his chest, unable to even look at his friends.

"Yes, Campbell, she did. I was spoken to by three ladies as I took my leave of the ball this evening. I do not doubt that, by tomorrow, everyone will be whispering about my declaration of love for Lady Margaret. Lady Farlinger has been telling her friends how ardent I was in my affections and how heartbroken I was at her refusal." Taking a sip of his brandy, he continued. "This is all to benefit her daughter, of course, to make her appear the most desirable young lady in all of London. Mayhap, upon hearing this, a Duke will pay attention to Lady Margaret, and thereafter, her betrothal to this Marquess will end."

Lord Dennington lifted an eyebrow.

"It is not like you to speak so harshly."

Given the dark mood he was in at present, Adam did not care.

"You were not present to witness how mockingly Lady Margaret looked at me, nor were you there when I was forced to stand and accept sympathies over my supposedly broken heart." With an effort, he lifted his head and looked at his friends. "You did not hear the dismissiveness with which Lady Margaret, and now Lady Farlinger, spoke of my affections. It seems that I am going to be mocked over my declaration, and that leaves me all the more frustrated, especially since I feel no lingering affection for the lady. Indeed, I am quite certain that there is no such thing as a true affection. Love is an imagined emotion without any real substance."

His friends looked at each other, then returned their attention to him.

"I do not think that you are speaking or thinking clearly," Lord Dennington stated, as Lord Campbell nodded fervently.

"Indeed, none of this is your fault. To have affection for a young lady is quite common, I am sure."

Adam shook his head.

"Mayhap it is, but it is certainly *not* common to discover that the lady in question is quick to dismiss such notions, I think."

"Certainly, it is not. When the time comes and you find yourself in such a position again, then I am sure that the response you receive from the young lady will be the exact opposite of that you received from Lady Margaret."

With a curl of his lip, Adam's jaw tightened.

"You may say so, but I do not think you can speak with any certainty on the matter. You cannot know the mind of every young lady in London."

"You *are* in a dark mood." Lord Campbell shrugged and looked away, letting out a long sigh. "That is to be quite understood, I am sure, but all the same, you ought not to permit yourself to have no hope. Lady Margaret treated you poorly, certainly, but that does not mean that *every* other young lady will treat you with such inconsideration."

Adam snorted.

"You do not think that I will ever permit myself to have such feelings again, do you?" He shook his head dismissively. "I will *not* allow myself to be drawn to another young lady again. I have already been mocked once. I shall never be so again.".

"Now wait for just a moment." Lord Dennington put one hand to his arm, but Adam shook it off. "You are responding to this much too severely. I thought you desired to marry a young lady who truly had an affection for you, and you for her. Pray, do not allow that desire to fade simply because of Lady Margaret."

Squaring his jaw, Adam looked away from his friends. They were trying far too much to encourage him, and he did not want to hear it at this present moment. Rather, he wanted only to sit in the shadows and allow them to settle over him.

"Lord Campbell is quite correct." Lord Dennington picked up his glass and took a sip before spinning the remaining liquid around in the glass. "Lady Margaret was the exception. Not every young lady is like that, I am sure."

"And what would you know of it?" With a sharpness to his tone, Adam twisted his head back towards his friends. "Neither of you have been eager to court a lady– although for different reasons, certainly. Neither of you are wed, nor even betrothed! How can you speak with any certainty about these *supposed* young ladies who will be willing to fall in love with me? As far as I am concerned, they are just as likely to be as Lady Margaret was. I could have no trust in them."

At this, Lord Dennington's brows dropped low as Lord Campbell's eyes flashed with a sudden spark.

"You need not speak so harshly to us." Lord Dennington's brows pulled even lower as Adam scowled. "We seek only to aid you."

Adam thought to say more, anger beginning to burn through him, but instead, he snapped his mouth closed and rose from the table, just as his anger began to bubble into shame. He had done wrong, he knew, but he was not in the correct frame of mind to even think about how to apologize for such a thing.

"You are quite right, I am nothing but disagreeable."

With a tilt of his chin, he turned his gaze away. "Excuse me, I think I shall make my way home."

He paused for a moment, wondering if either of his friends would encourage him to remain but, instead, they looked at each other and said nothing. Embarrassed now by his foolishness, and frustrated at his foul temper, Adam stormed out of White's to discover that dusk had fallen. Taking a breath, he made directly for his carriage.

"Would you like a copy of 'The London Ledger'?"

Something was waved in his face, and Adam snatched at it without even looking. Reaching his carriage, he climbed inside, the footman shut the door, and within only a few moments, they were pulling away.

Whatever is this?

With the aid of the lantern hung inside the carriage, he looked down at 'The London Ledger', and his gut twisted. This was simply society gossip, was it not? What would he find within? Tension clasped hard at his stomach as he leafed through the pages, searching for his own name. Would Lady Margaret's mother have spoken of him so loudly, already, that it would have gone into such a publication? He had hoped that his profession of love to Lady Margaret would remain between them but, then again, he had hoped for a lot of things and been disappointed in them all.

"'I search for a love match'?" Suddenly distracted, he found himself reading a letter within 'The London Ledger'. It was by an anonymous young lady who, it seemed, wanted to know whether any gentlemen in London sought the same type of match as she did. With a roll of his eyes, Adam folded up the Ledger, only to find himself thinking upon the letter. Muttering in exasperation to himself, he unfolded the Ledger and read it once more only to fold it up again. The purpose of his search was to find his *own* name, not to become distracted by something entirely banal. Once he reached the safety of his townhouse, he would read 'The London Ledger' again in its entirety... although should he find his name contained within, Adam was not certain what, if anything, he could do.

~

I CAN HARDLY BELIEVE that I am reading this.

Shaking his head, Adam looked down at 'The London Ledger' and read the letter contained within for what was now the fifth time.

"'I write in the hope that there will be some gentlemen within London who seek a marriage of love and affection, as I do.'" Reading aloud, he muttered the words into the empty space of his study. "'I am a young lady of quality, with an excellent dowry and a father who holds a high title. I do not wish to marry for convenience, nor to marry someone of my father's choosing, but desire a match where, at the very least, there is genuine consideration and affection. Therefore, if you are a gentleman seeking such a thing, perhaps you might write to 'The London Ledger' so that your response can be given to me. I write anonymously, however, knowing full well that there will be many who will take great amusement in reading this letter, no doubt laughing at my attempts to secure such a thing. To my mind, however, this is of the greatest importance, and it would be foolish for me not to do so. Therefore, if any part of my letter resonates with you, if it touches your heart, then pray write to 'The London Ledger' so that I might then consider you.'"

Scoffing, he shook his head, then threw the Ledger down onto the table. It was not in the least bit sensible for the young lady to have used the Ledger for such an endeavor for, after what she had written, he was convinced that many a gentleman would come professing their hopes for the same as she while, if they were true to it, they would confess that they cared only about her dowry and family title.

Getting up from his chair, he poured himself a whisky and then returned to his desk. After what he had endured with Lady Margaret, and now with being mocked in such a ridiculous fashion by her mother and by those close to her, his heart was heavy and painful.

Mayhap I should advise this young lady of the foolishness of her endeavors. Finding a blank sheet of paper, he uncapped the inkwell, lifted the quill from its stand, and began to write.

His response was not unnecessarily cruel but stated things as he saw them, quite clearly. It did not answer the young lady's question but rather told her in no uncertain terms that she ought to give up such an idea, for it was foolishness itself, and that gentlemen who responded would only be eager to know of her dowry and family title. He wrote as his heart told him, grieved and upset as it was, with every word as blood taken from his veins. Finishing the letter, he read it over again and, with a wry smile, sealed it with wax and rang for the butler, throwing back the rest of his whisky as he waited.

The edges of his vision blurred a little.

"Ah, there you are." When the butler stepped into the room, Adam waved the letter at him. "Tell me, do you know who writes 'The London Ledger'?"

He did not even think about the lateness of the hour and was a little frustrated when the man took a few seconds to answer.

The Butler blinked, then eventually answered.

"Yes, my Lord, I do." A slight frown pulled at his forehead. "I do hope that everything is quite well, my Lord?"

"I am perfectly well," Adam told him, hearing the slur beginning to creep into his words. "It is a publication that speaks only of gossip, is it not?"

Much to his surprise the butler hesitated.

"I would not say it contains *only* gossip, my Lord." The man spoke slowly as though he did not want to contradict Adam. "From what I know of it, Lady Yardley is very conscientious as to what is placed within the Ledger. The only time that there is ever gossip is when it is of benefit to those in the *ton*. In addition, it is always stated as such. If it be a rumor, then it is said to be a rumor."

A little surprised. Adam frowned then shrugged.

"Regardless, it does not matter. I should like this delivered to the writer of 'The London Ledger'. What did you say her name was?"

"Lady Yardley, my Lord."

"Then to Lady Yardley, at once." The butler went to leave, only for Adam to call him back. "It is not to be said that the letter comes from this house," he finished, firmly. "Do you understand?"

The butler nodded.

"You wish to remain anonymous, my Lord."

"Yes, that is it precisely." Getting up from his chair, Adam once more reached for his whisky. "Very good."

The butler left without a word and, moving from the desk to the window – though he could see very little through it - Adam sipped at his whisky, letting his thoughts wander. Why should this young lady of the *ton* be so eager for a love match? After his dealings with Lady Margaret, Adam could fully believe that very few of the *ton* were interested in such a thing. Ladies required the very best of gentlemen, as Lady Margaret had said herself, and thus would say whatever they wished if it secured a gentleman of high standing. While this young lady might very well be genuine in her hopes, Adam was quite secure in his belief that she was one of the very few within society seeking out such a thing. Perhaps some young ladies pretended to search for a love match, whilst inwardly hoping that it would be the highest titled gentleman, or the wealthiest fellow, who would come to steal away their heart.

I am convinced that, for the young ladies of London, it is a good deal easier to fall in love with a gentleman who has a great deal of wealth as opposed to a gentleman who suffers with a little less.

With a sigh, he threw back the rest of his whiskey and then strode across the room to pour another. He was already in a difficult frame of mind and reading that particular letter had only darkened it still further. Whoever this young lady was, he could only pray that she gained her senses again very soon.

CHAPTER SIX

"*A*nd has he introduced you to any particular gentleman as yet?"

Constance shook her head, watching as her father made his way directly across the room away from her.

"No, not as yet." Her stomach twisted into a tight knot as she kept her eyes on him, seeing him stop to talk to three gentlemen in particular. "Although, I am sure that he intends to, very soon. My mother has warned me that he has been in deep discussions with some acquaintances."

Wincing, she smiled briefly as Lady Brookmire let out a sigh.

"That must be difficult to hear. If you perhaps make some suggestions, would he then-"

"No, he would not." Understanding what her friend meant, Constance shook her head again. "My father does not desire to hear anyone else's opinions, save for his own. He will, on occasion, listen to my mother, but that is very rare indeed. I am afraid that, even if I were to complain and cry over the fact that my sisters were given ample opportunity to find their own husbands – who, of course, were required to garner my father's approval before even courtship was offered, he would do nothing but shrug. I am to accept my fate regardless of how I might feel about such a thing."

Lady Brookmire's expression grew a little dark.

"How painful for you."

Trying to ignore the stab of upset which sent tears to her eyes, Constance took in a long, shallow breath.

"I should be more grateful, mayhap. I am all too aware that my father has done a great deal in offering to secure me an excellent match. There must be many a young lady who would be delighted to have such an opportunity, whereas I find myself practically weeping over it!"

"But that is because you do not desire a practical match." Lady Brookmire smiled reassuringly. "There is no shame in that. You are not to think badly of yourself because you seek a little more." Again, she sighed. "There must be *something* which can be done."

Again, Constance sighed, pushing away her thoughts.

"There is not. I am conscious of Lady Winterbrook's suggestion, but while I have considered it, I do not think that there is any real hope for me there."

Lady Brookmire kept her own counsel, her lips tightening, her eyes moving around the room as if she were searching for an answer.

"Oh goodness." Constance reached out, clutching Lady Brookmire's arm. "My father is coming towards us. Look, he brings a gentleman with him."

"And I shall remain here with you." Lady Brookmire linked her arm through Constance's as if they were chained together in solidarity. "Recall that you are not standing up in church with this particular gentleman. All you are doing is greeting him."

"But I have no doubt that is my father's intention."

"Then let it be so." Lady Brookmire responded, unequivocally. "Do not let your mind go to that particular place as yet. Calm yourself. Speak firmly but respectfully. Show this gentleman, whoever he is, exactly the sort of person you are. He may decide that *he* does not wish to have you for a bride if you do so."

Constance looked to her friend in surprise, seeing Lady Brookmire's sparkling smile and finally understanding precisely what she meant. With a giggle, she nodded and then set herself to the task.

"Constance." Lord Hayman shot a glance at Lady Brookmire and, recognizing her, smiled. "And Lady Brookmire, good evening."

"Good evening, Lord Hayman." She turned a little. "And good evening, Lord Timpson."

Lady Brookmire spoke first, and Constance watched with interest as the gentleman's eyebrows lifted a little. Evidently Lady Brookmire was already acquainted with this gentleman, which was something of a relief. Perhaps she would be able to tell her more about him once her father had departed.

"Might I present my daughter, Miss Constance Millington." Lord Hayman spread out one hand towards Constance, then looked directly at her. "Constance, this is Viscount Timpson."

As was expected, Constance curtsied and greeted the gentleman as warmly as she could while, at the same time, taking him in. He was a good deal shorter than her father, which meant she considered herself almost of a height with him. Broad-shouldered and with a strong jaw, sharp eyes, and dark brown hair, she had to admit that he was not particularly unpleasant to look at. When he spoke, however, she was a little taken aback at the gruffness of his manner. Every word seemed to be rasped from his throat.

"Miss Millington, good afternoon."

His eyes dropped downwards as they ran the length of her frame, then returned to her gaze. Constance went red hot at the shame of his actions. What was he doing? Considering whether or not she would be beautiful enough for him?

"A very pretty thing." Lord Timpson spoke as if she were not present, and Constance ran hot all over again. "And hoping to wed?"

"Yes, that is so." Her father waved one hand. "She is the youngest of my daughters, but still has an excellent dowry, you understand."

Constance did not know what to say, words piling up in her throat – and when she tried, the only thing that came out was a squeak.

"I believe that this would be your third marriage, would it not?"

Lady Brookmire's clear voice broke through the conversation and Constance's heart leaped in surprise just as Lord Timpson coughed harshly, uncomfortably shuffling his feet.

"Your third?" Lord Hayman twisted his head around from Lady Brookmire to Lord Timpson, one hand lifting upwards in a questioning gesture. "I thought you told me your wife died."

"She did." Lord Timpson coughed again, then looked down at the floor. "My *first* wife, yes. The second, however... I was required to divorce her."

The audible gasp which came from Lord Hayman made Constance break into a smile. She had no doubt that Lord Timpson was considered no longer suitable for her. Divorce was thought of as the most improper thing, and Lord

Hayman would not want his daughter, nor his name, connected with a divorced gentleman.

"Father, Lady Yardley has arrived. Might I be permitted to go and speak with her?"

There was a brief silence whilst it took Lord Hayman some moments to look at her, for he was far too busy glaring at Lord Timpson.

"Yes. Go."

Not needing any more encouragement, Constance hurried away, Lady Brookmire still beside her.

"Oh, my dear friend. I am so very grateful to you!"

"Not in the least." Lady Brookmire chuckled quietly, throwing one glance over her shoulder. "It is very helpful when one is already aware of certain gentlemen. My husband has spoken to me of Lord Timpson before, for there were some business dealings which went awry also. Lord Timpson will have told your father that his wife died, certainly, but he surely will not have said anything about his *second* wife, simply because of the shame divorce brings. Divorce is not something any gentleman wishes to have attached to his name."

"All the same, I am very relieved and grateful to you for speaking so." With a sigh of contentment, she straightened her shoulders and stood tall. "Let us hope that something similar might be done with whoever my father decides to push toward me next!"

Lady Brookmire laughed softly.

"You never know, you may find yourself enamored of the next gentleman," she teased as Constance shook her head. "He may turn out to be the very best of gentlemen, after all!"

CHAPTER SEVEN

*T*he lingering pain in his head did not encourage Adam's heart to free itself from the doldrums into which it had sunk. He scowled and grimaced as he muttered through his various letters and invitations. It was not as though he were not pleased to be invited to such things, only that his headache had made him irritable and cross. With a sigh, he continued to write various acceptance letters or send his regrets. The very last invitation he looked at, however, made him pause. It was an invitation from Lord and Lady Hayman. The name seemed to bring something to mind, and while he struggled to recall it, he studied the invitation a little more. It was to be an evening ball at their townhouse, in celebration of their daughter's coming out.

It was then that recognition came. Miss Millington was, of course, the young lady he had spoken with a little over a sennight ago, and with whom he had danced some two days ago at a magnificent ball. That was when he had found himself in better spirits before news of Lady Margaret's betrothal and her mother's gossip had reached him. Since that time, this dark, muted mood had settled upon him and had not left him, even after a night of rest. Perhaps a ball at Lord and Lady Hayman's, alongside Miss Millington, would bring a little lightness back to him. After all, from what he recalled, she was a very charming young lady, and he had been delighted with her company. They had danced together and had enjoyed excellent conversation – and he had found himself admiring the red shimmer to her hair and the gold in her hazel eyes. They had not shared anything in depth, of course, but he had enjoyed her company regardless.

Perhaps this evening would be a pleasant one, so long as no one asked him about Lady Margaret!

It was with lifted spirits and a sudden lessening of the pain in his head that Adam wrote his reply. Yes, he stated, he would be very pleased to join them and was grateful for the invitation. His correspondence thus completed, he was about to rise and ring the bell, only for the butler to tap at the door.

"Lord Campbell, my Lord."

Adam blinked but nodded, directing the butler to the stack of letters just as Lord Campbell stalked inside. His friend was frowning heavily, looking from one place to the next, his eyes downcast and seeming entirely disconcerted over some matter. It was most unlike Lord Campbell to be at all displeased about anything, for his manner was usually very jovial and good-humored, so to see him now, his brows knitted together in such a fashion, was a little worrying.

"Campbell." Adam gestured for him to sit down, but his friend shook his head, continuing to pace about the room. "Something has troubled you." The memory of how he had spoken to his friends the previous evening slammed down upon him and guilt had him looking away. "I must tell you how sorry I am for my manner last evening. I can only apologize for my sharp tongue and dark mood."

Lord Campbell shook his head, then sighed.

"You were a little irritable last evening."

"I allowed my frustrations to push into my heart," Adam admitted openly. "And yes, I was in a very dull frame of mind. I am sorry for speaking so harshly."

With a nod, Lord Campbell opened his mouth, but then closed it again, continuing to walk up and down the room as Adam watched him with careful eyes. Whatever was troubling Lord Campbell, it seemed to be very serious indeed.

Eventually, Lord Campbell spoke.

"I have been informed this morning that Lord Westerton has returned to London."

Adam's eyebrows lifted high, his heart thundering in his chest. For, the previous Season, Lord Westerton and Lord Campbell had been at odds with each other, and Lord Westerton had behaved in a most inappropriate manner and had treated Lord Campbell very poorly indeed.

"I am sorry to hear it."

Lord Campbell closed his eyes, his jaw pushing forward as he curled one hand into a tight fist, his knuckles white as he came to a standstill.

"I thought I would have forgiven him by now - forgiven *her*." His voice was low, as though he spoke to himself, and Adam looked away, suddenly uncomfortable with his friend's vulnerability. It was not that he found what was being said disconcerting, but that he was uncertain as to how to respond. What could he say that would offer Lord Campbell any sort of encouragement? What could he say to a man who had been so broken by another? Lord Campbell had been betrothed to one Miss Barrett, but when Lord Westerton had come to London society, she was soon caught up with him instead and, after only a fortnight, the betrothal between the lady and Lord Campbell had come to an abrupt end. The excuse given had nothing to do with Lord Westerton, of course, but Lord Campbell had been all too aware of the truth. "It is not as though she ever declared herself to have a deep affection for me."

"But that does not mean that you did not have an affection for *her*."

Lord Campbell shook his head and sighed heavily.

"What is worse - and you will mock me for this, I am sure - is that my heart still longs for her in a way I did not expect." Adam blinked in surprise, but said nothing, choosing to wisely keep his thoughts to himself. His first impulse was to throw up his hands and state precisely what he felt about Miss Barrett and what she had done to ruin Lord Campbell's happiness. Why a gentleman should still find himself so inclined towards a young lady who had hurt him so furiously was not something he could understand. "Lord Westerton's return is not the cause of my strife, however." Lord Campbell groaned aloud, throwing back his head as he did so and continuing to pace up and down, no longer looking at Adam. "She is here."

This time Adam could not contain his surprise.

"You mean to say that Miss Barrett is back in society? She is in London?"

"Yes. She has returned with her mother and younger sister." Lord Campbell swallowed hard. "She is not wed." This was said with a sharp look sent in Adam's direction, but Adam simply shook his head in astonishment. He had expected – as Lord Campbell had also – that the lady would wed Lord Westerton. "Neither is her younger sister. I confess that I am astonished to hear that she has not yet married Lord Westerton. I thought that was the intention."

"We did not hear of any betrothal, I suppose."

"That is because I did not want to hear anything about her," came the sharp retort. "Do you recall? I forbade you from speaking her name. Lord Dennington, on the other hand, decided to forget that he had made me such a promise and told me about her return this morning."

Adam nodded slowly, rubbing his chin for a moment. Now that he thought of it, he did recall that his friend had stated such a thing last Season, and thus he had closed his ears to anything regarding the young lady and assumed that Lord Dennington had done the same. Now, however, it seemed that Lord Dennington had been the one to break their promise – although Lord Campbell did not appear angry about that.

"Perhaps it is a good thing that you know," he considered aloud. "You will be prepared for when you must lay eyes upon her again."

"Am I that much of a fool to still be drawn to her?"

It was a question Adam had no intention of answering, and as Lord Campbell continued to wave his arms around and expound at length, he sank back into his chair and let his friend speak openly and without interruption. Lord Campbell talked of how his heart had been sore, grievously pained, and how he had found himself to be in such a dire situation that he had believed he certainly could never allow his heart to feel an affection for anyone again. But despite a year passing, he still found himself thinking about her. Yes, he had told himself repeatedly that it was foolishness and stupidity, and that he was nothing but a fool, but upon hearing of her return, much to his frustration, his heart had leaped about with a sudden joy - a joy he did not wish to feel.

This, Adam concluded, was again a reason why

allowing oneself to fall in love was quite ridiculous. It would do nothing but bring heartbreak and sorrow, frustration, and confusion. How glad he was that *he* would not permit his own heart to settle upon such a thing again!

"And thus I find myself quite at a loss; still in love with a young lady I want to forget."

Adam sighed heavily.

"And I believed you last evening when you told me that you had no feelings for her, although I should never have made such a remark as that either."

"I lied." Lord Campbell threw up both hands, his voice echoing around the room. "I knew it would be seen as foolish and, given the heaviness which already hung upon you, it was not as though I wished to have it thrown like a cloak over my shoulders also." Flinching, Adam sank back into his chair a little more. What Lord Campbell said was quite true, for he had been in a very despondent mood and had never once thought how his manner might affect his friends. "Besides, how could I admit such a thing to you, when I could barely admit it to myself?" Now, eventually seeming to lose some of his strength and no longer pacing the room, Lord Campbell made his way towards Adam and then slumped into a chair opposite. "I know myself to be a fool, but what else can I do but confess it, in the hope that in telling you of it, it may leave me?"

"And has it done so?"

Rising, Adam went to pour his friend a whiskey. Yes, it was very early but, to his mind, the situation required it.

"No."

Sounding most irritated, Lord Campbell took the whiskey from him with a grunt.

"I do not think you are a fool." Adam shrugged both

shoulders. "Though I do think that you ought to attempt to rid yourself of these feelings in some way."

"As you have been able to do, so easily?"

Adam turned away, making to sit back down in his chair.

"Yes, I have been able to remove the affection from my heart easily enough," he stated quite honestly. "But in all truth, I begin to wonder whether love is a truly genuine emotion that one can feel for any great length of time. Mayhap *some* can, such as yourself but, on the whole, I begin to consider it an emotion that is easily dissipated."

At this, Lord Campbell snorted aloud and rolled his eyes.

"You say such things only because you have never *experienced* love."

With a scowl, Adam drummed his fingers on the edge of the table, aware of the hint of temper beginning to rise.

"How can you say such a thing to me? You know very well I had a great depth of feeling for Lady Margaret."

"Feelings which came only from your fortnight with her." There was a slight scoffing tone to Lord Campbell's words which had Adam recoiling inwardly. "That is not love. You may believe it to be so, but I can assure you it is not."

Adam shook his head, thinking to argue, only to remind himself that this discussion was not about his feelings for Lady Margaret, but rather about his friend's affection for Miss Barrett.

"Then if love is what *you* are experiencing at present, I do not wish to have any of it within my heart. I can see how much it tortures you and certainly, I do not want to be so bound."

"And you have become cynical about it also, I see."

With a sigh, Lord Campbell threw back his whisky and then set the empty glass down, shaking his head when Adam lifted one hand in the direction of the bottle. "No, one is enough. I thank you." He took another breath. "Let us end our discussion on love. I think it is a little fruitless and certainly not what I require at this moment."

A little embarrassed at his own thoughtlessness, Adam nodded, aware of the prickling of his skin and flush running up to his face.

"What is it that you require from me?"

Lord Campbell looked back at him steadily. His chest rose and fell as he took a long breath, considering before he spoke.

"I require you to keep me away from Miss Barrett."

Blinking a little in surprise, Adam tilted his head.

"Whatever do you mean?"

"I mean precisely that." With a shrug, Lord Campbell looked away, his face coloring. "My desire is for the lady, and thus I have every assurance that I will no doubt wish to speak with her, desire to dance with her and the like. I *cannot* be permitted to do so, for then my heart will become quite overwhelmed and no doubt, lost to her forever. If you see me watching her, direct my attention elsewhere. If you see me speaking with her, then join our conversation. In doing so, you will remind me of what she did and, I hope that will cause me to then move from her side. In time, I hope that my feelings will fade to the point where I have no desire to be in her company for anything but brief moments..." Groaning, he ran one hand down his face. "At present, the only place I desire to be is beside her."

"I can do that."

Lord Campbell nodded but did not smile.

"I thank you. I will be asking Lord Dennington to do the same, also, of course."

Allowing a small smile to spread across his face, Adam shrugged his shoulders.

"Mayhap I shall be exactly what you require."

"Whatever do you mean?"

Again, Adam lifted his shoulders.

"Given that my thoughts on love are that it is nothing but foolishness, I shall be quite firm in presenting you with the reality of your situation. No, indeed, you do not need to concern yourself. I shall be precisely the person you need to assist you in removing all thoughts of Miss Barrett from your mind."

At this, Lord Campbell managed to smile, the first smile Adam had seen since his friend's arrival.

"I suppose I should be grateful." The quietness of his voice expressed his profound sorrow over his feelings for Miss Barrett. "Although you may discover, in time, that your assumptions about love are quite wrong. Once you truly fall in love with someone, it is almost impossible to rid yourself of them. Time supposedly makes an end of it, but I silently believe that now, such a love lingers in your heart for the rest of your days. It may only be a small measure, as a reminder of the time when your heart had filled up entirely, but it shall always linger there; a single drop where there was once a fountain."

"Most poetic." Adam got to his feet, dismissing the latter part of his friend's statement. "Come now, let me ring the bell and we shall have a feast sent up to us. We shall rid that sorrowful look from you, one way or the other."

With a seemingly great effort, Lord Campbell managed to smile, although it fell away quickly.

"An excellent idea." With a breath, he pushed himself out of his chair. "Thank you, old friend."

Adam returned his smile with a nod, putting his hand on Lord Campbell's shoulder.

"But of course. It is the very least I can do."

CHAPTER EIGHT

"*L*ook, is that Lord Seaton approaching?"

Constance's heart leaped, but she quietened it at once. She had enjoyed their first dance together some days ago, but he had not come to seek her out since. For whatever reason, her heart had lifted at even the mention of him, as if she were very eager indeed to be in his company again. Recalling her mother's wide-eyed look and Lady Winterbrook's suggestion regarding the gentleman being a Marquess, wealthy and perhaps eager to fall in love, Constance's cheeks warmed as he came to speak with her; her mother melting away into the shadows.

"Miss Millington." Lord Seaton inclined his head, his smile lingering. "I believe that we may have to dance again this evening if that does not trouble you?"

Constance laughed softly.

"It seems that dancing is what one does at a ball, my Lord."

Lord Seaton's answering laugh had Constance's breath quickening, for his blue eyes lit with a sparkling light when he did so, and she found herself thinking him to be *very* handsome.

"I do hope that you are eager to give me your dance card?" Quickly, she slid it from her wrist and handed it to him. One eyebrow rose. "Very eager, it seems."

His twinkling smile made her laugh.

"And again, Lord Seaton, I would remind you that it is the requirement of every young lady to dance as often as she can at occasions such as this."

The smile danced in his eyes.

"That is quite true, I suppose. I think I shall take two of your dances, so you might have an evening full of nothing but such an entertainment."

"How very kind of you."

Constance could not deny that her heart rose in a thrill of delight as he handed her back the card. She glanced at it quickly, attempting to find his initials, but could not. Almost all of her dances were now filled, but she did not want to appear rude by searching eagerly for his name.

"I have not danced the waltz in some time, I confess." Lord Seaton shrugged. "Let us hope that it is not a disaster!" Her breath caught as she lifted her gaze to his face, then dropped it back again to her card, searching through her dances, wondering whether or not he spoke the truth. Was the daughter of a Viscount truly to dance the waltz with a Marquess? Finding his initials there, her breath came out in a loud sigh and warmth immediately poured into her face. "You are displeased?"

"No, not in the least!" Searching for an explanation, she dropped her hands to her sides again. "It is only that I have not danced the waltz in some time either." Her heart beat furiously, the words sticking in her throat. "Perhaps we shall be the most embarrassing of couples, and then what shall we do?"

Thankfully, her words were taken as gentle teasing, and Lord Seaton grinned back at her.

"That certainly would not do! Therefore, we must hope one of us is able to dance acceptably."

"Indeed!"

Her composure returned, and she smiled at him, only for it to fade away as her eyes caught her mother returning to them. Evidently, the private conversation had gone on long enough.

"Lord Seaton." She smiled warmly as he bowed. "How very good to see you again, and under better circumstances also!"

Much to Constance's relief, Lord Seaton chuckled.

"Lady Hayman. Yes, I am doing no injury to your daughter, I can promise you."

"I am very glad to hear it!"

Lady Hayman laughed as Constance resisted the urge to sigh and turn her head away, a little embarrassed.

"I was hoping that either Miss Millington or I would be able to recall the steps of the waltz," Lord Seaton continued, as Lady Hayman's eyebrows lifted high as she turned her gaze towards Constance. "It has been some time since I danced it, but I look forward to stepping out with Miss Millington."

"As I am sure she will be glad to step out with you." Her mother then looked directly towards Constance, her gaze growing fixed until Constance was forced to murmur that yes, she was looking forward to it very much. "Although I was sorry to hear of your recent disappointment." Lady Hayman sighed. "That must be very difficult for you." Constance frowned, then glanced at Lord Seaton only for her breath to swirl in her chest. Lord Seaton's expression had grown cool, his jaw a little tight. When he smiled, there was not even a hint of happiness in his eyes. Whatever it was that her mother was talking about, Lord Seaton was clearly not at all eager to discuss it. "I am assuming that this will not set you back for the rest of the Season, however?" Lady Hayman continued, evidently entirely unaware of the effect her words were having upon the gentleman. "There are *many* young ladies in London more than willing to tie themselves to a gentleman such as yourself."

Lord Seaton coughed lightly, then clasped his hands behind his back as tension thrummed through the air between them.

"Yes, of course. You are quite right." He said nothing more, and silently, Constance begged her mother to remain silent also. Whatever it was they were discussing, it was clear that Lord Seaton had no desire to speak of it himself. Thankfully, she finally managed to catch her mother's eye, at which Lady Hayman merely laughed and clapped her hands together, shattering the strain. "Forgive me, I will not interrupt your conversation any longer. Do excuse me."

Lord Seaton nodded, murmured a good evening, and then returned his attention to Constance, whilst still clasping his hands behind his back.

"I will take my leave of you also. I am sure that you have many other gentlemen to dance with, and I should not like to intrude."

Urgency rose like a fire within her.

"Wait a moment." Without thinking of what she was doing, Constance put out one hand on his arm. "I do hope that my mother did not embarrass you in some way. I confess that I do not know what she spoke of, but I can see that it was a little distressing for you. I can only apologize on her behalf."

Lord Seaton immediately twisted his head away, his shoulders lifting in a shrug.

"It is nothing of consequence, at least."

Allowing his shoulders to relax, he threw her a glance and then, with a nod of his head, stepped away.

Constance's heart sank as he walked away. She was aware that he had felt distinctly uncomfortable and unsettled at what her mother had been speaking of. What was it that had caused Lord Seaton so much distress? How embarrassing that her mother had behaved so! Had she truly not seen that Lord Seaton had no wish to discuss the matter?

"You are to dance with Lord Seaton, then?"

Starting a little, Constance smiled with relief as Lady Yardley looked at her.

"Yes, I am."

"And there is no sign of Lord Timpson either."

At the mention of that particular gentleman's name, Constance rolled her eyes.

"No, indeed. Did Lady Brookmire tell you of it? I was so very grateful to her for her aid."

Lady Yardley chuckled.

"Yes, she informed me of how white Lord Timpson went when she spoke of his marriages." Her smile slowly faded. "Though I have been considering how I might be of aid to you in this."

"Of aid to me? In what matter?"

"Why, in the matter of your father and his decision to find a husband for you." Lady Yardley laughed as Constance smiled, a little embarrassed. "And I think there is something I might do."

Saying nothing, Constance waited for her friend to continue her explanation.

"Being the author of 'The London Ledger' has its advantages." Lady Yardley's smile stiffened. "Although it can also be something of a burden. I know a great deal about the *ton* and those within it... both the good and the bad."

Constance's eyebrows lifted.

"And you think you might be able to speak against any gentleman my father considers? Just as Lady Brookmire did?"

"It could be a small thing that I might be able to push into gargantuan proportions." Lady Yardley lifted one shoulder. "I do not think your father would read 'The London Ledger', however."

"I think you are correct in that," Constance answered with a wry smile. "My mother might be inclined to do so."

"I have a better idea." Lady Yardley gestured across the room. "You need to introduce me to your mother. Whatever I say to her will no doubt be passed to your father."

"Yes." Speaking slowly, Constance hesitated. "Though I cannot be certain he will give it much credence."

Lady Yardley shrugged.

"Then I will speak to him myself, if I must."

Constance's eyes flared.

"You would do such a thing for me?"

"Certainly, I would." Lady Yardley squeezed her hand. "Both myself and your friends would do anything required to make certain that you have as much opportunity as they had to find a love match."

Tears threatened, but Constance blinked them away, happiness and relief warming her through.

"Thank you, Lady Yardley. Come, let me introduce you to my mother at once."

THE THOUGHT of dancing the waltz with Lord Seaton had been difficult enough, but now she was standing up with him, the prospect was utterly overwhelming. She had not been entirely truthful to Lord Seaton, for while it was quite true that she had not danced the waltz in some time, the only person she had ever danced it with had been her dancing master. Having never been in a gentleman's arms, she now found her confidence to be shattering into tiny pieces on the floor.

"The music begins." Lifting his head from a bow, Lord Seaton stepped forward. "And now we are to prove to the *ton* that either we *can* recall the waltz and can dance it perfectly, or," he continued, one hand going to her waist, "we shall show ourselves to be the very worst dancers in all of London, and shall become a laughing stock."

Constance tried to laugh, but the sound became trapped, her tension rising so rapidly that she was breathing very hurriedly before the dance had even begun. Was this how it felt to waltz with a gentleman? Was this why her heart was so flooded with delight?

The music took them away together and there was suddenly no more time to think. Lord Seaton led her through the dance, and she went with him, only for her anxiety to begin to fade away, unraveling itself behind her as she was turned all around the dance floor. Lord Seaton too fell silent, for while it was usual for there to be a little conversation during the dance, on this occasion it seemed that neither of them could speak. Constance looked up into his eyes, watching him as he led her this way and that with great confidence. She did not even have to think about what she was doing, for they moved effortlessly together, and perhaps, she considered, he too might feel the same delight as she did at this moment.

His eyes were like the sky when the very first stars appear, a light shining from within them. There was no smile on his face, yet his eyes danced, and Constance became entranced. It was as though he pulled her into his spell, the power of his presence capturing her. She did not care in the least bit about anyone else, did not care a jot that her mother would be watching her with sharp eyes and, no doubt, a delighted smile. She forgot about Lord Seaton's teasing about their dance steps, and forgot her own worries, for there was nothing *to* fear, not when she was dancing with Lord Seaton.

"It seems as though I did not fail you."

The dance was over before she felt it had even begun. When he bowed and released her, she stumbled a little, falling backward and forcing Lord Seaton to grasp her arm to steady her.

"Forgive me." Mortified at her own lack of composure, she slid her arm from his hand but grasped his fingers instead, using his strength to aid her as she curtsied. "I will admit to being a little dizzy."

"I quite understand." With a smile, Lord Seaton offered her his arm. "The waltz can induce such feelings, I think. One does not go around and around and around without consequence!"

Relieved at his understanding, she laughed and put her arm through his, allowing him to lead her back toward her mother.

"You certainly did not let me down, Lord Seaton. I believe that was the very best waltz I have ever danced."

Managing to regain herself, she offered him the heavy compliment, which he accepted with a broad smile while being entirely unaware that she had not danced the waltz with any other gentleman as yet.

"How very kind of you to say so. I am personally delighted that it went so very well." His eyes found hers, his smile softening just a little, his voice a little quieter also. "I do hope that it is a dance we can repeat on another occasion. Let it not be our last waltz together, Miss Millington. I should very much like to step out again with you soon... but only if that is something which would please you."

The smile on his face now faded entirely, his eyes widening a little as if he were afraid that her answer would be negative.

"Yes, it would. I should be truly delighted."

With a sudden leap of her heart, she smiled up at him and, as she gave her eager reply, Lord Seaton's smile returned with such brightness, it stole her breath. Lord Seaton was, she considered, handsome, amiable, gentle, and kind.

Perhaps the sort of gentleman I might find myself in love with after all.

CHAPTER NINE

"You have had some replies." Lady Yardley beamed as Constance caught her breath, her hand flying to her mouth. "Goodness, I did not think you would be so surprised! It is just as I expected." Rising, she walked across the room to a small table and took from it a silver tray, which held a small stack of letters. Bringing it to Constance, she set it down on the table between them. "You see?"

"I am *truly* delighted." Constance clasped her hands together so that she would not reach out to take the letters from the tray. "How many have there been?"

Lady Yardley laughed quietly.

"Many more than this, but from the seals upon some of them, I knew at once that the gentleman who had written the letter would not be genuine in their desire so, thus, those letters were removed from the group you see here."

Constance nodded eagerly, not in the least bit frustrated.

"Yes of course. I quite understand."

"I am relieved to hear it. Thus, I have narrowed these

letters down to six. I am sure more will come, but these are the six I suggest you read to begin with. I have not read them, of course, but have left them sealed for your eyes." Lady Yardley gestured to the ones on the table. "They are all for you, and the seals are from gentlemen of the nobility, all of whom have excellent reputations."

Leaning forward, Constance picked up the first, only to turn it over and see that it had no seal at all pressed into the wax.

"And what of this?"

Lady Yardley frowned.

"That is one I do not know about." Her head tilted "The address here is written by a very fine hand, but there is no seal on it. I did not want to hold it back from you since it is addressed to you, but might I suggest that you read it with great caution. I cannot be certain of what is contained within." She shrugged. "Or mayhap it will have the gentleman's name and I will be able to tell you whether he is worthy or not."

Constance nodded, then chose to set it aside. Picking up the next letter, she broke the seal and spread it open, relieved that it was only Lady Yardley and herself present at this moment. While she appreciated her friend's willingness to be of assistance, she did not want them to coo over every letter she received. It would be up to her to decide which gentleman she would pursue - if any.

"This first one is from Lord Humphries." She read the few lines, then smiled. "He is very brief, but he states that he has been searching for a bride for some time. He has said that his only requirement is that she has a heart open to all matters of love."

Lady Yardley nodded, then shrugged.

"Lord Humphries is a worthy gentleman, certainly,

although he is a little older." Her lips pulled flat as though she were struggling not to say anything more than that, but Constance noticed the tight expression regardless.

"I should not like to determine a gentleman's worth simply by his age, if that is what you mean."

With a chuckle, Lady Yardley shook her head.

"No, indeed, and I congratulate you on your lack of judging... though you may change your mind when you see him." Lady Yardley giggled, sounding a little like a young lady at the beginning of her first Season, who laughed and teased about the various gentlemen in London, and Constance too was caught up with laughter. Lady Yardley was so very pleasant, so easy to converse with, it was as though she spoke with a very dear friend whom she had known since childhood. "Here, then." Handing her the next letter, Lady Yardley smiled. "This is from Lord Warrington. He is a Viscount, like your father. He has an excellent hold-ing, although he does live in Scotland."

"I do not think that would be any particular difficulty." Constance lifted her shoulders. "If I find a gentleman who loves me, then why does it matter where he resides?"

"Precisely."

Lady Yardley beamed as if she concurred exactly with everything Constance had said thus far. As she broke the seal and unfolded the letter, Constance blinked in surprise at the numerous lines which were written within. His writing was very small, so he could fit as many words in as possible, and it took her some minutes to take in everything which he expressed.

"He is a gentleman who likes to articulate each and every feeling, I think."

"Oh?" Lady Yardley gestured to the maid who had just come in with the tea tray, to set it to one side so it would not go anywhere near the letters. Her eyes rounded when Constance held up the letter so that she could see the plentiful words. "I do not know if he is like that in conversation, though he is perfectly suitable."

"Then it would be wise for me to consider him." Constance murmured as she held the letter out. "Should you like to read it?"

Lady Yardley accepted the letter from her.

"I do not think I would have the time." With a smile, she chuckled softly. "My goodness, Lord Warrington *has* written a great deal. Perhaps he is eager to express the fervency of his emotions."

"Perhaps." Taking up the third letter, Constance broke the seal and unfolded it carefully. She leaned towards Lady Yardley so that they might read the lines together, although this time, there were only a few. "And this from Lord Blayton. I am not acquainted with him."

Lady Yardley nodded sagely.

"Another very suitable fellow. He has an excellent town house and a wonderful estate near London. He is also something of a dandy, but such things could change once he is wed. And mayhap such a thing would not provoke you in the least."

"I could not say – not until I met him, I think, although I am sure it would not be so."

Constance found her heart so thrilled that even the suggestion of some difficulty had her shaking her head. No, she would not allow herself to become overwhelmed by this. Whichever gentleman it was that wrote to her, she was glad for each of them. Living in Scotland or having a great many words with which to express himself, or being a little of a dandy did not cause her any real distress. If these gentlemen were all seeking love matches, then she would give each of them some of her time in the hope that she might find herself falling in love with one of them.

"And here we have the fourth."

The fourth and the fifth letters presented no real difficulty in any way, and Constance was delighted to read them both. They expressed the same desire as she- a desire to find a marriage where love was at the center. She caught herself smiling so strongly, her cheeks began to hurt.

"Perhaps we have here, in one of these gentlemen, the one you shall marry."

Constance nodded and made to say that, yes, she hoped so, only for a sudden face to come to her mind.

The face of Lord Seaton.

All at once, she frowned and looked away, rising to pour the tea, even though Lady Yardley had not asked her to do so. Whyever was she thinking of Lord Seaton? Yes, he was a gentleman of her acquaintance, and certainly, they had been in company a little more of late. She found him amiable, genteel and, given that he was a Marquess, his title held great standing, but that did not mean that she ought to be thinking of him at this present moment! It was very odd indeed.

"Are you quite well, Miss Millington?"

"A little overwhelmed." Constance handed tea to Lady Yardley, who thanked her, and then took her cup back with her, resuming her seat. "This has proven a good deal more exciting than I imagined it would. And in addition, my father has stated that he has no other gentleman to introduce me to as yet." Her eyebrow lifted as Lady Yardley grinned. "I am sure that I have you to thank for some of that. Did you say much to him?"

"I have been conversing with your mother – who I like enormously, I must say – and she informed me of your father's next gentleman under consideration. His next *two*, in fact. I was relieved to be able to state something disagreeable about them both, although I may have emphasized one a little more than was required." With a laugh, Lady Yardley beamed, as if she were truly delighted with herself. "I am glad to know he has listened to your mother."

"As am I."

Constance smiled, just as Lady Yardley's eyes went to the final letter on the table.

"We have not read this mysterious letter as yet. Do you wish to?"

"Oh, of course."

A whirlwind of anticipation blew around her as, for the final time, she broke the seal and spread out the letter, expecting there to be yet more of the same - an expression of a kindred spirit and a similar hope.

Instead, her heart crumpled in on itself as she read the few short lines. They were not spoken with any great darkness, nor a desire to cause pain, but rather spoke in clear, sharp statements. First, the letter told her that her desire for a match of affection was simply foolishness. If there was such a thing as a genuine love between two people, it was entirely by chance and could not be expected to grow simply by the word of someone alone. Love in itself, he said, was most likely a fleeting emotion, and easily removed from oneself. Secondly, this gentleman practically berated her for stating that she had a suitable dowry and came from a titled family, with a highly regarded father at the head of it, for *that* was what gentlemen sought out. Thirdly, he told her, those who responded and claimed to be seeking the same as she was, were not telling her the truth. They sought her dowry, her beauty, her family status, and nothing more.

He did not sign his name and, as she finished her reading of the letter, tears began to sting her eyes.

"Good gracious, Miss Millington!" Lady Yardley set her tea down quickly, making the cup rattle in the saucer as she got to her feet. "Whatever has happened?"

"You may read it for yourself if you wish."

A little surprised that tears were now clogging her throat, she handed the letter to Lady Yardley and, blinking rapidly, picked up her tea again, attempting to dismiss the sharp pain which had plunged so deeply into her heart.

Lady Yardley sat back down slowly, reading the letter carefully.

"Goodness, this is nothing but brokenness speaking," she said, firmly, looking back at Constance. "Whoever this gentleman is, he writes from a place of pain, I think." Her voice was quiet, although her eyes narrowed a little as her gaze returned to the letter. "Although why he should think to take upon himself such a task as this is quite beyond me! Mayhap he believes that he is doing you a great service in telling you that you ought to disbelieve any gentleman who desires to find a love match, but I can assure you that he is quite mistaken."

She made to crumple the letter, but Constance, for whatever reason, found her hand stretching out for it again. Lady Yardley returned it to her with a slight frown, but Constance could not give her an explanation. Her eyes ran over the words again.

"He says here that love is nothing more than a fleeting sensation." She read the letter again, relieved when no tears came to her eyes this time. "I am astonished that any gentleman should think that writing this particular letter would be of any use to me. Clearly, he desires to make me believe that love is not something worthwhile, that it is something not worth seeking."

"Yes, I believe that is precisely what he intends." Lady Yardley sighed and shook her head before picking up her tea again. "You must forget about that letter. It is worth nothing more than the heat it will bring you when it burns in the fire." Smiling, she reached across to touch the five letters Constance had left out on the table before them. "*These* are what you should be considering. Set your thoughts upon the gentlemen you are to meet instead of the one you ought to ignore!"

Constance took a deep breath, set her shoulders, and smiled.

"Yes, you are quite right."

As she looked at the letters again, each one professing her desire, she realized that her heart ought to be singing. Strangely, however, her thoughts turned again to Lord Seaton. It was as though he were desperate for her attention, as if he were forcing himself into her mind and her thoughts, even though she did not want him there. More than a little confused, she took a deep breath and gave herself a slight shake, just as Lady Yardley smiled.

"I suppose the very first question I ought to ask you is, which gentleman do you wish to be introduced to first?"

Constance tugged her thoughts away from Lord Seaton with a great effort.

"I do not know. I am not acquainted with any of them, so I shall require introductions to them all."

"Then why do we not begin at the first?" Lady Yardley gestured to the first letter. "And you must assure me that if your father brings to you another gentleman, or suggests another fellow whom he thinks *more* than suitable, you will tell me of it immediately."

Seeing all that Lady Yardley was willing to do for her, Constance could not help but smile.

"I certainly shall, and I am so very grateful to you for all of your help in this matter." Her gaze returned to the five letters. "I have hope now, and I must pray it will bring me what I have always longed for."

CHAPTER TEN

*A*s Adam stared across the room, he found himself weighted to the floor. He could not explain it, for it was not the first time that he had looked upon the young lady, but now that he saw her again, it was as though his entire being was somehow pulled towards her. At the same time, however, the desire to remain precisely where he was, almost in fear of what he now felt, grew strong.

Thus, he simply stood.

He had set his eyes upon this young lady many a time. To see her now laughing and smiling was precisely what he ought to expect, for that was what almost every other young lady in the ballroom was doing. He had seen her eyes before, had seen her smile, had held her in his arms. So why now should he find himself suddenly so transfixed?

"If you are going to gaze at a particular young lady, I should like to know her name."

Lord Dennington's broad grin and nudge had Adam wincing and he turned away sharply, suddenly freed.

"I am doing nothing of the sort."

"Yes, you are. Why? Who were you looking at?"

Adam cleared his throat, hoping to change the topic of conversation.

"I hear that you spoke to Lord Campbell about Miss Barrett." Lord Dennington simply lifted an eyebrow and Adam sighed inwardly, folding his arms across his chest and shrugging. There would be no escape for him. "Very well. I was merely thinking how well Miss Millington looks this evening."

He had no other choice but to admit to it, for his friend would not permit him to remain silent nor would he change the subject of conversation until he found out the truth. Yes, Adam could have named any young lady, but the desire to be truthful was strong.

"Miss Millington," Lord Dennington repeated as Adam nodded, glancing over his shoulder, and then turning away, as if he were now entirely disinterested in her. "You have danced with her before I think?"

"On a few occasions."

"And do you find her good-natured?"

"She is just as any other young lady." Adam shrugged as Lord Dennington grinned, his eyes twinkling at Adam's attempts at nonchalance. "She is amiable, kind, good-natured, with easy conversation and a beauty of her own."

At this, his friend began to chuckle.

"My goodness, Seaton! You tell me that you were in love with Lady Margaret, and how determined you are not to ever allow such emotions again. You say that you believe them fickle and without strength. But now, look how quickly you have found someone else to consider?"

"I do not dote upon her." Adam snorted and looked away, tilting his chin as he did so. "I simply saw her as I entered this evening and thought I would consider her for a moment."

He did not mention the fact that his heart had skipped wildly, nor that he had found himself stuck in one position and had been unable to move. That was for his own considerations and given that he was utterly confused over why he had responded so, it seemed wise not to tell Lord Dennington of it.

"She is the daughter of Viscount Hayman, is she not?"

"I believe so." Adam sniffed, then looked back to Lord Dennington. "Now, of Miss Barrett. I did think that—"

"And do you intend to dance with her this evening?"

Adam opened his mouth and then snapped it shut as Lord Dennington's grin grew.

"I do not think it matters whether or not I intend to dance with one particular lady."

"I should say it does." Lord Dennington tilted his chin in Miss Millington's direction, over Adam's shoulder. "For she is already encircled by at least *four* gentlemen, and I am sure that if each of them took two dances, her entire dance card might be filled very soon."

Despite his attempts to state to Lord Dennington that he had no specific interest in Miss Millington, Adam whirled around at once, only to see Miss Millington standing with her friends, as she had been only a few moments ago. With a groan of exasperation, he looked back towards his friend, but Lord Dennington simply shrugged, then laughed aloud.

"I was simply thinking she was a very likable young lady, that is all." With a loud sigh, he grimaced. "Now speak to me of Miss Barrett. What is it that we are to do?"

Lord Dennington frowned, his mirth quickly forgotten.

"Lord Campbell has asked us to inform him about whether or not Miss Barrett is here this evening. I believe that, if she is, then he fully intends to go in search of the card room, to make certain that he does not go anywhere near her. I believe he may wish to permit her a passing glance or two, solely to show her that he has not been entirely broken to pieces by her betrayal... or to make certain that he is able to trust himself. "

"While, at the same time, battling a desire to grow close to her again." Adam shook his head. "I confess I do not understand that."

"That is because you have never truly loved a young woman as Lord Campbell has done," he said calmly and quite seriously. "Trust my words on this - when you find yourself so enthralled by someone that you cannot, simply cannot, even seem to *breathe* without thinking of them, *then* you are in love. What you felt for Lady Margaret was an infatuation, or the beginnings of genuine affection... nothing more." Upon saying this, he did not allow Adam to argue, turning on his heel and moving away as he spoke his final words. "Now, if I were you, I should make my way to Miss Millington's side as quickly as possible, for it seems quite certain that she will soon have her dance card filled."

Believing that his friend was teasing him yet again, Adam could not help but turn his head around and look to where Miss Millington was standing. To his surprise, she was, in fact, now speaking with two other gentlemen and a third was approaching.

What if I cannot dance with her this evening?

A sudden urgency had him taking hurried steps towards her, strangely aware of his strong desire to have at least a few moments with her in only his company. To be able to dance with her would provide him with such an opportunity, and he could not let it slip by. This only added to the strange sensations and confusing emotions which wound through him but, pushing all that to the side, he inclined his head and coughed gently, making certain to garner her attention.

"Miss Millington." Fully aware that he was interrupting the conversation of the other gentlemen, Adam threw them both a quick glance, shrugged, and then continued his conversation. "I was hoping I might take your dance card before it has no space left upon it."

Miss Millington did look particularly beautiful this evening, he considered. The gentle pink in her cheeks, the light in her eyes and her warm smile made his own lips curve in response. Yes, he realized, he *did* want to be in her company this evening. He would have to simply disregard Lord Dennington's teasing.

"Good evening, Lord Seaton." Her slightly lifted eyebrow had a flush creeping up his neck. "As you may notice, Lord Kingsbury has my dance card at this present moment, though I am certain he would be glad to pass it to you when he is finished."

"I should be very glad of it."

Adam held out one hand in Lord Kingsbury's direction, seeing how the gentleman frowned, and then quickly returned his gaze to the dance card. It was, to Adam's deep frustration, that he then saw the gentleman writing his name down for the only waltz of the evening. With a sigh, he took it from the fellow, then proceeded to write his name down for two separate dances, the cotillion and then the country dance. Neither of them were what he wanted, for he had hoped to dance the waltz with her, but they would have to suffice. Besides which, considering the strange urge to be in Miss Millington's company this evening, mayhap he ought to take a little time to consider what he was feeling at present. It was entirely disconcerting and a little alarming since he had already declared that he was going to refuse to allow his heart to feel any sort of affection for any young lady ever again.

With a brief smile, he handed the card back to the lady, only to jerk his hand away when their fingers brushed. The thrill that moment provided began to remind him of a time past when he had been caught up with Lady Margaret. Surely this was not the beginning of a *similar* sensation for Miss Millington? He could not permit himself that!

Adam frowned heavily.

Mayhap I ought to have withdrawn rather than pushed forward. A heaviness settled upon him. *Surely I will not be so foolish again so soon.*

Scowling, he excused himself, citing that the other gentlemen required her attention now and he would return very soon to claim his first dance with her. Shaking his head to himself at his own foolishness, he caught sight of Lord Campbell standing a little further away and, with a small sigh, went towards him.

"You cannot be looking for her already." Lord Campbell said nothing as Adam lifted an eyebrow. His friend was leaning against one of the stone pillars within the ballroom, a drink in his hand but his gaze sweeping across the room from one side to the next. "Campbell?"

"I do not need to search for her. She is already here. Lord Dennington told me so only a few minutes ago."

Adam nodded, frowning just a little.

"Then ought you not to be gambling? Staying far from her."

Lord Campbell's jaw jutted forward.

"I shall go there soon. Do you see her? She is dancing with Lord Poncily."

"So now you have seen her, is it not time to turn away from her?" Adam tried to smile, but his friend only scowled all the more. "Come now, what else did you expect from her?" His smile fading, Adam spoke a little more sharply. "It is not as though she is going to attend every ball and refuse to dance, is it? She is, as is every other young lady in London, seeking a match. I am sorry it was not with you but–"

"Why then did she not marry Lord Westerton?" Lord Campbell's voice was dark. "She was transfixed with him. It was plain for all to see.

"But he was not enamored of her, mayhap." Taking a breath, Adam chose his words carefully, trying to speak as gently as he could. "It is the state of things, is it not? One must feel an affection or a delight in one's chosen suitor, while the suitor must also feel such an affection in return. Mayhap Lord Westerton did not feel such a thing and thus, there has been no match made between them. It is now required for her to begin all over again and find someone new."

Lord Campbell snorted.

"Unless, as I am, you find yourself still drawn to the one person who has caused you such pain," he stated with a wry smile. "Yes, yes, I suppose what you are saying is quite true, and I am aware of how foolish I am to desire to seek her out again. And yet, despite knowing all of this, I cannot remove myself from this place. I cannot stop watching her dance."

"I must beg your pardon."

To Adam's surprise, none other than Miss Millington was standing just behind him, her gaze dropping away, her cheeks flushed and obviously a little embarrassed to have interrupted them.

"Miss Millington."

"I do not mean to intrude upon your conversation, but it is time for our dance, Lord Seaton."

Adam blinked quickly. Had that time arrived already? He had not expected it to be so soon but, then again, he could not even recall what dances he had secured from Miss Millington.

"Oh, of course."

"Although your friend looks a little troubled." Miss Millington put a hand on Adam's arm for a moment. "I shall not insist. Our dance is of very little importance."

"Of course, you must dance." Lord Campbell, clearly having overheard the conversation, smiled and then inclined his head towards Miss Millington. "My dear lady, I quite insist that you have your dance together."

Miss Millington had not removed her hand from his arm, and slowly Adam began to feel a gentle warmth spread from where she held him so lightly. It was not he that she looked at, however, but rather at Lord Campbell, which, strangely enough, added only frustration to Adam's heart. Pushing that irritation down, he turned and instantly, Miss Millington's hand dropped from his arm.

Regret flooded him.

"Come, Miss Millington, let us do as Lord Campbell says, and stand up for our dance."

Eager for the touch of her hand again, he offered her his arm and, with a smile, she took it.

"Very well, Lord Seaton, but as long as you promise to bring me back and introduce me properly to your friend." Her eyes twinkled and both Lord Campbell and Adam himself smiled. "Formal introductions are quite important, I think."

"I quite agree." Lord Campbell chuckled and then nodded to them both. "I look forward to being introduced to you very soon."

Without any further ado, Adam led Miss Millington to

the dance floor, his embarrassment reigniting over the remembrance that *she* had come in search of him so that they might step out together.

"I am afraid you must forgive me, Miss Millington, for my forgetfulness in coming to seek you out."

Much to his relief, Miss Millington only laughed.

"Oh, pray do not concern yourself, Lord Seaton. It was not any trouble, for in all truthfulness, I wished to remove myself from the conversation of one very ardent gentleman and was glad to have an excuse!" It was on the tip of Adam's tongue to ask her which gentleman this was, but given that she did not offer his name, he chose to remain silent. Besides which, why should it matter to him who it was? Gentlemen were bound to be interested in Miss Millington's company. She was quite delightful in every way. "So you see, you did me a great favor."

Her hand pressed his arm lightly and Adam's heart suddenly soared, only for heat to burn in his face. A warning rose in his mind, a warning that he was allowing himself to feel far too much for this young lady... but try as he might, he could not rid himself of such emotions.

The dance permitted them a good deal of time for conversation, and as they stepped together, Miss Millington enquired as to Lord Campbell and his seeming distress.

"He does not seem to be a gentleman in particularly high spirits this evening, which is somewhat unusual, is it not? Given that a ball is always such a joyous opportunity for conversation and laughter."

"I believe he is a little... heartsore." Making certain to speak carefully, for he did not want to give all of Lord Campbell's situation voice, Adam thought quickly. "It is a matter of the heart, I believe."

"I see." She did not smile any longer, her expression

now a little thoughtful. "I have heard that such things can cause a great deal of distress. I am sorry for it."

"That is very kind of you." Adam smiled at her, silently thinking of just how sweet a nature Miss Millington appeared to possess. "I am sure that he will recover himself in time."

"We must hope so." Miss Millington spread out her hands and tilted her head as the dance came to a close, their hands releasing from one another. "I have heard that these things can take a good deal of time to recover from. I have no experience of it myself, I confess."

"Nor have I. I-"

The words died away as he frowned, but Miss Millington, dropping into a curtsey, did not see it. Was that truly how he felt? No longer able to state that he had been desperately in love with Lady Margaret and now suffered ongoing pain over their separation?

That is because it was nothing but a moment. A brief love that faded easily.

His lip curled. Did he truly believe that love was a fleeting emotion, one which held no substance, able to be pulled away at any given moment? How, then, could he explain what it was his friend now suffered with if it was not a broken heart?

"You now appear rather thoughtful." Miss Millington settled her arm through his as they returned. "I do hope our conversation has not brought any difficulty to you."

Quickly, Adam shook his head.

"No, not in the least," he promised, thinking it was not something he wished to share when it came to his experience with Lady Margaret. "It is only that I do find myself concerned for my friend. I wonder if he will ever recover. He seems very unlike himself."

"Perhaps I might talk to him?" Miss Millington lifted her shoulders. "I would be glad to. Mayhap I know the lady he is besotted with and might be of aid to him in how to best seek out her affections."

"Forgive me, but I do not think that would be wise." Adam pulled his lips to one side for a few moments. "This will sound very strange to you, I am sure, but he does not desire to feel this way about this lady. *That* is where the confusion lies, you understand."

"I see." Miss Millington's eyes darted up to his and then away again. "All the same, if he would be willing to speak with me, then–"

Their conversation lapsed into silence as they approached Lord Campbell. Miss Millington smiled warmly and after a moment, the gentleman returned it.

"Might I present Miss Millington, daughter to Viscount Hayman." Adam quickly made the correct introductions. "Miss Millington, this is my dear friend Viscount Campbell."

"From Scotland, of course." The gentleman chuckled, then inclined his head. "I am delighted to make your acquaintance."

"As I am glad to make yours." Miss Millington smiled warmly, her voice soft. "Though I was sorry to hear about your present difficulties. You need not look so sharply at your friend, however, for Lord Seaton has not given any secrets away, only to say that you have been a little sorrowful of late."

"And in that regard, he is quite correct." Lord Campbell sighed and shook his head. "I will not pretend this has not been painful. My heart is quite trapped, Miss Millington. Perhaps you might know of a way to help me release it."

Adam looked at Miss Millington, a little surprised at

how openly his friend spoke, having only just been introduced to her. Perhaps, he considered, it was because Miss Millington had such a pleasant demeanor about her, and that made conversation particularly easy.

"I am afraid that I know very little about matters of the heart." Miss Millington leaned against Adam for a moment, and it was then that he realized her arm was still through his. "Might I ask why you wish to remove your affection from this lady?"

Lord Campbell laughed harshly.

"You may well ask." He flung out his hands. "It is because the lady in question quite tore my affection from me. She made a mockery of it through her actions, though she would probably not say so. I found myself alone when I ought to have been wed. Does that suffice, Miss Millington?"

She nodded and Adam, glancing at her, caught the glisten of moisture in her eyes. Did she truly feel such a great depth of emotion for Lord Campbell's circumstances?

"And do you say you still care for this young lady, even though she has treated you so ill?"

"Yes, it is precisely so." Lord Campbell closed his eyes briefly. "And so, you see, I am quite without hope."

"Unless it is that your heart holds to her for *another* reason." Miss Millington lifted her shoulders. "As I have said, I know very little of such things, but rather than attempt to push away your affection, does your heart not lead you back towards her?"

"But she has done him a great wrong!" Adam protested, turning slightly so that her hand fell from his arm. "I do not think that you understand the depths of his pain."

"I am certain that I do not." With a soft smile, Miss Millington looked towards Lord Campbell again. "But I am sure that love, if that is what it is, can truly find a way through such difficulties. It may be that this young lady regrets whatever it was that separated you. If there is a hope of your connection returning, Lord Campbell, then would you not be best to seek it out?"

Adam made a low exclamation in the back of his throat, but Miss Millington did not so much as glance at him. She and Lord Campbell simply looked at each other with Lord Campbell frowning and running one hand over his chin, as if he were considering her suggestion. A little frustrated, Adam looked away, his jaw tight. Miss Millington was, to his mind, giving the worst sort of advice to his friend. Lord Campbell did not require someone to encourage him back towards Miss Barrett. Instead, he required someone to push him away from her, for that was what he himself had demanded. Besides, Adam thought to himself, the idea that love was strong enough to push through such difficulties and to forgive great pain was more than ridiculous – which, yet again, was another reason to eschew the very idea. He thought very little of the notion of being in love, thinking to himself that he would never even *dream* of approaching Lady Margaret again.

"Alas, I must depart." With a small sigh, Miss Millington gestured across the room. "My mother, who has been watching me for some minutes, is moving in such a way as to make me fear that she will come to join us and I should not like to interrupt your conversation any further."

Adam nodded, a little surprised at how quickly his irritation faded, disappointment rising to quench it.

"Should I accompany you?"

With a quiet laugh, Miss Millington shook her head.

"I would not subject you to that, Lord Seaton."

With a quick curtsey and a warm smile to both Lord

Campbell and him, Miss Millington took her leave. Letting out a long breath, Adam watched her depart, then turned back to his friend.

"She does not fully understand your pain, although I know she meant well."

Lord Campbell shrugged.

"She did offer an alternative perspective."

A little astonished, it took Adam a moment to respond.

"That may be true, but do you think moving back towards Miss Barrett is a good idea? You asked the very opposite from both myself and Lord Dennington, did you not? You asked us to make sure that you were pulled away, so that you would *not* be drawn any further back towards her."

"That *was* what I said," Lord Campbell agreed, quietly, "but part of me wonders now if Miss Millington is correct. Perhaps what I feel for Miss Barrett remains so strong, it will make up for the pain and the sorrow I have struggled with. Perhaps it will be enough to encourage our connection once more."

"You are speaking foolishness." Without hesitation, Adam spoke firmly, wanting to pull his friend away from what he considered to be nothing short of desperation. "She has proven herself false once, and I am certain she will do so again. Do not injure yourself in that way. It is as though you are taking a knife and by your own hand, plunging it again into your heart."

"Or mayhap I am the one withdrawing it."

His expression was so very different from how Adam had seen him some minutes ago, to the point that he could not find a way to respond. The last thing he desired was to bring the darkness back to Lord Campbell's face but, at the same time, he felt the urge to draw his friend away from the path he now seemed determined to take.

"Do not hold me back this time." Lord Campbell's gaze pulled away from Adam as he spoke quietly but with great fervency. "As you have said yourself, I begged you to pull me away from her, but on this occasion do not do so. The very least I can do is speak to her. It will push away some of the tension which spirals between us, I hope."

Concern flew into Adam's heart, and he put out one hand as if to physically pull Lord Campbell back, but he was much too late. Frustration pooled within him as his friend moved quickly across the ballroom, directly towards Miss Barrett. Adam could do nothing but watch helplessly, a little perturbed that Miss Millington's advice had been what had pushed Lord Campbell in a very different direction. If only she had remained silent, then none of this would have happened.

CHAPTER ELEVEN

"Lord Dalrymple." Constance dropped into a curtsey, looking desperately around the ballroom in search of one of her friends, or Lady Yardley, in case any could come to her aid, but none came into her view. "I am very pleased to make your acquaintance."

This was, of course, not truly what she meant, but without any other choice as to what she ought to say, she could only offer the required platitudes and hope that something altogether untoward about Lord Dalrymple would soon reveal itself. The ball had been so very enjoyable thus far, particularly when she had waltzed with Lord Seaton, but now, was it to be ruined by her father's attempts to push another gentleman towards her? A knot tied itself in her stomach. What if her father demanded that *this* gentleman, Lord Dalrymple, was to be her betrothed? What would she do then?

A slight dizziness took hold.

No. I must remain strong. I must make my feelings clear regardless of how much Father is displeased with me.

"We have been long acquainted, Lord Dalrymple and I."

Lord Hayman lifted his chin a notch as if this was some sort of accolade.

"Is that so?"

At her dull, toneless voice, her father huffed out a breath in obvious warning, as Lord Dalrymple nodded, his third chin wobbling significantly. Beady eyes looked back at her as though she were a delicate piece of meat from which he intended to carve out a piece for himself.

"And *more* than suitable for the third daughter of a Viscount."

Lord Dalrymple chuckled as her father laughed aloud, as though suggesting that the gentleman had made a very good jest.

Constance, however, was appalled. Was this how her father spoke of her to others? As though she were lesser than his other two daughters simply by the placement of her birth? What of these gentlemen? Did they know anything about her character at all, or was it only *their* suitability that was considered by her father?

"She has, of course, had all the teaching and education required for a young lady." Lord Hayman gestured to her with a flutter of his fingers as Constance recoiled. "You will find her quite proper, I am sure."

"Very good."

Constance made a quiet exclamation, horrified at how her father was speaking of her. Lord Hayman smiled tightly but, unfortunately, the sound was caught by Lord Dalrymple.

"Is there something you wished to say?" His eyebrows lifted a little. "I thought you were quite well trained?! I did not think, therefore, that a young lady such as yourself would ever interrupt two gentlemen when they were speaking."

Constance blinked, then lifted her chin even though her heart was hammering furiously.

"I beg your pardon, but my father introduced you to me only a few minutes ago. Thus, we are *all* meant to be in conversation, are we not?"

Recalling what Lady Brookmire had suggested as regarded making herself appear a little less than perfect for any gentleman her father brought to her, Constance spoke firmly, but without being rude. Rude was not something she would ever permit herself to be, but she could show Lord Dalrymple that she was not a quiet, retiring young lady, even though her father might have painted her as such.

"This is most extraordinary!" Lord Dalrymple threw up one hand. "You can *clearly* see that your father and I are in discussion and-"

"Yes, you are both talking about me. Given that I am present and able to hear every word you say, I find the lack of consideration for my presence a little unbefitting two gentlemen such as yourselves." Her father's eyebrows rose, only to fall low over his forehead as he scowled, a flush rising into his face in clear annoyance over how she was behaving. Constance did not stop, nor hold herself back as, no doubt, her father wished her to do. Instead, she continued, speaking in as calm a voice as she could, while remaining firm in her expectations. "What would be better would be for you to speak to me directly. I can inform you about all that I have learned these last few years, and share with you my interests or the like. Indeed, I would be glad to speak with you, rather than have you talk as though I am not present."

She looked directly at Lord Dalrymple, aware that he

was frowning much as her father but almost relieved to see such an expression. Mayhap that expression meant that he would not think as well of her as her father wished him to

Lord Dalrymple scowled, then spoke, his low voice rasping.

"I do not need to ask *you* any such thing. If I want to speak with you, I shall state it clearly."

He threw out one hand and a rush of air flung itself across Constance's cheek, as though he had thought to prevent any further words coming from her lips. Constance stepped back, her stomach roiling. Had he almost struck her?

"Then I have no interest in you continuing your conversation with my daughter."

Much to Constance's astonishment, it was not Lady Yardley, nor Lady Brookmire who spoke, but her mother. Constance had not seen her mother since they had arrived at the afternoon soiree, for she had gone at once to speak with some of her friends, and left Constance with her father. Now, however, she had appeared just at the very moment that Lord Dalrymple had come close to striking her.

"I beg your pardon?"

Lord Dalrymple seemed just as horrified that Lady Hayman would speak in such a manner, looking to Lord Hayman for a moment before returning his gaze to Constance.

She stood tall, suddenly free of all anxiety. Somehow, she knew that her mother was here to defend her.

"Do you think that I should condone the acquaintance of a gentleman who thinks it perfectly permissible to behave in such a manner towards my daughter? Someone he has only just become acquainted with?" Lady Hayman tossed her head, her eyes flashing with a vehemence that Constance had never seen before. "I hope that you are not considering this supposed gentleman for our daughter, Lord Hayman. I certainly will not approve of it."

"It is not Lord Dalrymple who has failed, my dear." Lord Hayman's tone was quiet, but dangerous with it as well, warning his wife to stay quiet without saying so directly. "Constance interrupted our conversation."

"You mean that you were speaking about her, even though she is standing beside you? After you had introduced her?" Thrilled at her mother's support, Constance wondered just how long her mother had been listening nearby before coming to her defense. She wanted to throw her arms around her and embrace her tightly but instead simply stood quietly, smiling inwardly but keeping her expression quite clear. "How can you bring a gentleman to your daughter, introduce him, and then expect her to stand there in silence as you discuss her traits and suitability? That in itself is rudeness, and I am surprised to hear you defend such behavior. Surely for our daughter, you seek a gentleman who would show some interest in his wife?" There came a slight catch in Lady Hayman's voice. "Or do you intend to have a gentleman wed to our daughter who cares very little for her? Who thinks nothing of her opinions and cares not a modicum for what she has to say?"

With a tightness to her throat, Constance slid one arm through her mother's, recognizing that these words came from a place of personal distress. They stood together as Lord Hayman looked away, a deep flush rising into his face.

"I can assure you that, if you did such a thing, my Lord," the lady continued quietly, "Constance would not find herself in a happy marriage. That is not what you want for our daughter, is it? I am hopeful that you seek the very best match for her, as opposed to simply a suitable gentleman who might satisfy your *own* requirements."

It was the first time that her mother had ever spoken with such fervor, and Constance, still a little astonished, looked to her, only to see Lady Hayman's eyes glistening. Her heart ached, and she pulled herself a little closer. Her mother's hand came to her arm, and rested there as they stood together, fortitude against presumed strength, until, finally, the two gentlemen were the ones to buckle.

"I think I shall take my leave." Lord Dalrymple was the one to move away, ending their time together. "Despite our conversation, I do not think that there can be any connection between us, Lord Hayman. I am sorry."

"I am not."

Constance knew that she ought not to speak such things aloud, but after what she had endured, it came to her lips, and she did not hold it back.

"Constance!" Her father's eyes were flashing, his lip curling. "How dare you speak so? Do you have any understanding of what you have done?"

"I have done nothing other than be my true self, Father." Constance did not raise her voice, but spoke with great fervency. "Think for a moment of what you have placed upon me. Can you imagine what it is like to stand here and have you and a gentleman, whom I do not know, speak about me as though I am entirely absent? That you speak of my training and education but not of my character, as if I am a horse at Tattersall's or the like, and not a thinking person?"

"And besides which, my Lord, the gentleman almost struck your daughter. I am deeply upset to see your lack of response, for you appeared not in the least bit concerned about that, but instead choose to berate her as though she were the one at fault." Lady Hayman spoke with the same fierceness as she had towards Lord Dalrymple, her chin lifted high. "Your lack of consideration is both displeasing and concerning."

"This is foolishness."

Her father had never been as red in the face as he was at this moment, Constance was sure of it. She had never seen him so angry, so lost for words, and yet there was a confidence brewing within her which had only been encouraged by her mother's presence.

She wanted to say more.

"You have not given me the same opportunities as my sisters, Father." Taking a breath, she continued. "I say none of this to anger you, but only to make you realize that I will not be contented with a gentleman you present to me, simply because he is of your choosing. Do you truly think that someone like Lord Dalrymple would be suitable for me? Someone who tells me that I ought only to speak when he asks me to do so?" Softening her voice, she tilted her head. "Is that how you treat Mama?"

Before Lord Hayman could answer, her mother spoke up again.

"Certainly, it is not, so why should you want that sort of gentleman for your daughter? Do you not care about her happiness in the least?"

Lord Hayman opened his mouth only to snap it closed again. His eyes were sparking with obvious anger, but he said nothing, turning on his heel and stalking away.

The moment he did so, Constance felt her mother slump just a little, and turned to her with concern.

"Mother?"

"Forgive me, my dear."

A little confused, Constance looked at her.

"There is nothing to forgive, Mama."

"Indeed, there is." Lady Hayman turned slightly so that she could take Constance's hand. "I have been speaking to Lady Yardley of late and she has, in her kind way, made some circumstances plain to me. This fresh understanding has made me deeply upset." With a sigh, she closed her eyes. "It is unfair that your father did not offer you the same opportunities as he did your elder sisters. I can understand your frustration and your upset in that regard. I do not like his choice and I want you to be aware that I do not condone it." Her eyes opened and she looked directly at Constance. "Your father does not often listen to me, but I will do whatever I can to assist you in finding a good husband. That is why I came to join you when Lord Dalrymple was being presented to you, even though my heart was beating so furiously, I was sure that it would leap from my chest!" Constance smiled softly, tears in the corners of her eyes. Her mother had never spoken to her in such a way before and while she was grateful for it, she did not like the pain she saw in her mother's expression. "Make no mistake, my dear. I was silent before, but I will be silent no longer. Your father is not right to treat you in this lesser way and thus, I will make certain that you have my voice alongside you. I want you to be happy."

To Constance's horror, her mother's eyes welled up with sudden tears and she quickly squeezed her hands tightly.

"Pray, do not be upset on my behalf, Mama. I have spoken with Lady Yardley too, and she has aided me in my search for a suitable husband who might bring contentment to both Father and myself. That is not to say that I am not grateful for your aid also, but only to say that I have not been friendless these last few weeks."

"I can see that, but I ought to have spoken up from the very beginning." Lady Hayman blinked rapidly and, much to Constance's relief, her tears dissipated without falling to her cheeks. "But I shall be here with you now."

Constance's heart filled with both appreciation and love for her mother. Lady Hayman had always wanted the best for her daughters and, while clearly struggling with the strength of her husband, was now willing to do whatever she could to aid Constance. Thus far, two gentlemen of her father's choosing had been foiled, and his attempts to encourage them toward her had been entirely unsuccessful. She could hope now that such efforts would continue to fail until she finally found a gentleman who would hold her heart, and she would hold his.

"Miss Millington, might I present Lord Humphries to you."

Lady Yardley, upon making the introductions, took a small step to the side, looked at Constance, and smiled.

Constance's stomach dropped. Lord Humphries was not the sort of gentleman she had expected. He might very well be seeking a love match, but she knew at once that she would not be able to fall in love with him. He looked more suited to spending time with her father than with her, given his age. Yes, she recalled, Lady Yardley *had* informed her that he was a little older, but she had not expected him to be so very much so.

"It is very pleasant to make your acquaintance." Lord Humphries inclined his head, smiled, and then looked to Lady Yardley. "And how does your husband fare, Lady Yardley?"

"Very well, thank you." The lady smiled back at him. "He returned to the estate for a short while, but will come again to London soon. I know that he has greatly benefited from your advice about crop rotation."

"But of course! Have you heard of such an innovation, Miss Millington?"

She shook her head no and what followed was a long and seemingly inexhaustible explanation of crop rotations. Constance listened as best she could, attempting to take in all that was said and show, at the very least, a little interest. Thus far, Lord Humphries was not the sort of gentleman she would be able to consider. She had to hope that the next gentleman would be a little improved.

"Oh, you must excuse me." Lord Humphries, as though he knew her thoughts, waved one hand at someone over Constance's shoulder. "There is someone I simply *must* speak with."

Constance blinked.

"Oh, but of course." As he walked away, she sighed and sent a wry glance to Lady Yardley. "You did warn me, I know."

Lady Yardley laughed and smiled.

"Yes, I did, but I still think it was right for you to meet him. After all, he took the time to write a response to 'The London Ledger'."

"Though he is a little too old, I think."

"Yes, just a little." The laughter in Lady Yardley's voice made Constance chuckle and soon the two ladies were in fits of laughter. "There is something I would like to ask you." Lady Yardley finally managed to pull her expression straight as Constance blinked away the mirthful tears in her eyes. "You do not have to answer, of course, but I did wonder if there was any *particular* gentleman who had caught your eye?"

"Caught my eye?" Constance repeated, only to look away. "No, I do not think so."

"No?"

A glance back at her friend gave Constance the chance to catch a glint of interest in Lady Yardley's eye. Upon seeing it, her face grew hot, and she shook her head.

"Yes, I have been in company with Lord Seaton on occasion, but that is all there is at present. He does not show any particular interest in my company, although I do think him an excellent gentleman."

"That is because he *is* an excellent gentleman," Lady Yardley confirmed. "I have never heard anything but good about him. If you were to state that you had a little interest, there might be something we could place in the Ledger to confirm that his character is as we think? If you like, I could-"

"No. Please do not." A thread of warning running through her veins, she smiled, still a little embarrassed. "I am a great believer in having *both* the gentleman and the lady be as much in love with each other as the other. If Lord Seaton wished to spend more time in my company, would he not have come to call or asked to take a walk in the park together?"

Lady Yardley nodded.

"Mayhap." Her head tilted. "But it might also take a little time. Some gentlemen are inclined to slowness, you know." With a smile, she linked her arm through Constance's. "Now come, let us go and see if we can find another one of these gentlemen to introduce you to. I am sure you will find the next gentleman very handsome indeed."

Constance lifted her eyebrows, but Lady Yardley only smiled. Evidently, she knew precisely who she wished to introduce to Constance. But as she was being led willingly away, Constance found her thoughts returning to Lord Seaton. If he showed her even the slightest bit of interest, would her heart not cry out with both eagerness and antici-pation of spending more time in his company? Constance was all too aware of just how much she was enjoying his company, albeit only whenever they were at the same ball or soiree together. Every time he came to speak to her, every time they danced, her heart filled up just a little. Was there any hope of a connection?

Her smile fell.

It is foolishness to think so. Father will soon present me with someone he has deemed suitable, and all such thoughts might be lost.

With a small sigh, she steeled herself. It would be best not to admit to what she was feeling within her heart. That way, should the worst come to pass, her heart would not break and she would not be left with the dull memories of what it had been like to care for a gentleman.

CHAPTER TWELVE

"*I* believe that you have taken some of the gossip from me."

Adam offered Lord Campbell a wry smile as they walked together through Hyde Park.

"So it would seem." Lord Campbell was not smiling. Indeed, he had not smiled for at least a sennight, according to Lord Dennington's observations, and that did concern Adam somewhat. To his mind, this fresh melancholy had come upon his friend ever since Miss Millington's advice to him to go and speak with Miss Barrett. Thus, he was quite certain that the meeting had gone dreadfully, and that this was the reason for Lord Campbell's solemnness. "It is unfortunate that society is all too aware who talks with whom and who dances with whom, as well as being all too ready to bring up the history of one particular connection." With a sigh, Lord Campbell shook his head. "I do not like it."

In an attempt to be sympathetic, Adam cleared his throat gently, making sure to speak quietly.

"Might I ask how you are faring in this?"

Lord Campbell snorted.

"I am faring as anyone might," he remarked with a small smile, glancing over at Adam for a moment. "The *ton* is interested in my reacquaintance with Miss Barrett, while the only thing *I* am interested in is Miss Barrett herself."

Adam let out a breath, tension running up his spine to his shoulders.

"You mean to say that, as yet, your affection for Miss Barrett has not relinquished its hold up on your heart?"

"That is precisely it." Lord Campbell sighed heavily. "Though I confess that I am a little less inclined towards its disappearance now."

A small smile touched Lord Campbell's mouth as Adam twisted his head, shooting a sharp gaze toward him.

"Really? That has come about because you spoke to Miss Millington, has it not?"

Lord Campbell nodded.

"Yes, it has. I found her advice very different from what I thought I wished to do, and thus, understanding myself a little more because of her remarks, I now choose to do as she suggested. You may be surprised to hear it, but I believe that I find myself the better for it." There was no relief in Adam's heart over the statement. Instead, he simply shook his head. "You do not think me wise."

"I cannot, and will not, tell you what to do." Adam spread out his hands for a moment. "I am only concerned that you will be caused additional pain by following a path that brings you near to the lady again."

Lord Campbell shrugged.

"All the same, I am considering giving the connection a chance to flourish again, if she will have me." The shock of this ricocheted against Adam's chest and he had to fight to catch his breath. Seeing it, Lord Campbell chuckled. "I have shocked you again, I see."

"Certainly you have." Taking another few seconds, Adam swallowed hard before choosing his words carefully. "My dear friend, I must advise against it. That young lady injured you so severely, and in a way which does not seem to heal. Can you truly put yourself in danger of that again? Surely the injury this time will be so severe, it may be the end of you!"

Much to his surprise, Lord Campbell chuckled.

"You think that I shall fade away? Crumble to dust?" he suggested, as Adam grimaced. "I am not teasing you, my friend. I understand that your concern is genuine, but I must speak from my heart. Indeed, I am certain that I will wither away and die if I do not give my heart what it desires."

"And what does it desire?"

With a sigh, Lord Campbell smiled softly.

"It desires Miss Barrett, as it has always done." There was nothing Adam could say to this. After all, who was he to question a man's heart? All the same, he considered, this was nothing but foolishness. Yes, he was sure that what Lord Campbell felt was a deep affection that was true and sincere. But how could such a deep affection overlook such a great injury? It made very little sense and again, simply confirmed to Adam that to permit his heart such feelings would bring him nothing but sorrow and frustration. "You are not going to ask me what I intend to do, then?" Lord Campbell arched an eyebrow as Adam shot him a look. "I have been speaking with her, as you know."

"And what has she to say for herself?"

Lord Campbell chuckled.

"Very little other than to apologize," he told him, making Adam's surprise grow rapidly. "Miss Barrett is truly sorrowful over her decision. There is no obvious answer about whether she wishes to bring our connection back again but, certainly, she does want very much to express her regret."

"And you take her words to be truthful?"

"Of course I do." Lord Campbell shrugged his shoulders. "Why should I not?" Adam's expression answered Lord Campbell's question without him having to say anything. To his thinking, there could be many motivations for a young lady to apologize to a gentleman she had hurt. As yet, Miss Barrett was unwed and had not joined in matrimony with Lord Westerton, as had been expected - which meant that she was, again, looking for a husband. Would it not be easy enough for her to climb back into the affections of Lord Campbell and secure herself a very happy position without too much effort? After all, they had rubbed along together very well indeed before Lord Westerton's appearance. Perhaps she was hoping it could be so again. "You have your reasons to doubt her, I can see, but you will not speak them, though I can clearly see your disinclination towards trusting what she says." Lord Campbell rolled his eyes. "I do not know whether to be pleased or irritated."

Adam smiled gently.

"Believe me, my friend, you do not wish to hear all that I have to say."

"Then I suppose I should be thanking you." With a sigh, Lord Campbell closed his eyes for a moment. "Love is something you simply refuse to consider any longer, is it not? You have set your mind on the idea that all such affection, or even the *talk* of love, is nothing more than idiocy. You see it as being something which will only bring pain or detriment with it."

"And as a frippery." Adam remained adamant in his view of such things, not holding back the truth from his friend. "A word that is so often bandied about by many, but means very little to them. It seeks to capture those within its grasp and bind them until their hearts are either broken or their emotions have run dry." His shoulders lifted. "I wrote as much when I responded to the letter in 'The London Ledger'."

At this, Lord Campbell stopped short.

"'The London Ledger'?" he repeated with eyes wide with surprise. "I did not think that you read such a publication."

"It was thrust upon me," Adam answered with a slightly grim smile. "But... you must read it, for you appear to know what I speak of?"

Lord Campbell nodded.

"I do, on occasion. It can be lighter, and more entertaining fare than the usual newspapers. So yes, I did see the young lady's letter, seeking love. That is, I assume, the letter you refer to?"

"Yes, it is, and I did reply, and have not had any response in return, although..." Wincing, he looked away for a moment. "I may not have been in the very best state of mind when I wrote my response to it. I did write rather harshly. The specifics of which I cannot clearly recall, but I believe that I stated that the call for such a gentleman was idiocy and would bring the lady nothing but disappointment."

"Then let us hope that whoever wrote such a letter

receives many more positive replies and ignores your rather callous one."

For whatever reason – and for the first time since he had recalled what he had done - Adam began to wonder if he had done wrong. Guilt began to wind its way around his heart, and he frowned, heavily. It was a little too late to take back what he had written, but for the first time, he began to consider what the reaction of the young lady would have been when she read those words. Guilt pushed down heavily upon him, and he looked away.

"You did not consider her, did you? In your forthright-ness and determination to help the lady understand your perspective, seeking to have her think of it as the right one, you wrote without hesitation. I have no doubt that the young lady who wrote the letter, eager as she is to find a suitable love match, would have found your response very callous indeed."

Adam's jaw set and, for a moment, anger flared, but he cooled it quickly. His friend was not chiding him, but simply laying out before Adam exactly what would have happened once his letter had been received. Was that the sort of gentleman he was? One who wanted others to follow *his* views without hesitation, one who would force his harsh opinions upon them?

No, he did not want to be so.

"You are right." There was nothing Adam could say, save for that. "I was much too severe, I will admit. I should have simply read the letter and then let it fade from my thoughts. But given my state of mind at the time with Lady Margaret's rejection and subsequent betrothal, her mother's gossiping about my affections, and the heavy darkness I had pulled into myself, I chose to respond." His mouth twisted. "Mayhap I should write another letter, and apologize for the first. From what I recall, I did not sign my name to it, which would explain why I have had no response, so it remains entirely anonymous, which perhaps is to my benefit."

Lord Campbell hesitated, then spread his hands wide.

"It has been some time since the letter seeking a love match was published and, since then, two other Ledgers have been published. It is probably entirely unnecessary."

"All the same, I am grateful to you for pointing out my error." Adam wrestled with the strength of the guilt building within him. "Goodness, I have been a very dull fellow these last few weeks, have I not?"

"I would not say so."

With a jerk of surprise, Adam turned around just to see Miss Millington standing behind him. She laughed when his eyebrows lifted, and immediately he found himself smiling, his own heart beating hard within his chest.

"I do not doubt that my mother will accuse me of eavesdropping, but I could not help it. I saw that you were here, as we were walking, and thought to greet you." Miss Millington gestured to her left where her mother stood waiting, and Adam smiled and nodded at Lady Hayman. "But no, indeed, I do not think that you have been at all dull. I personally have been enjoying your company of late."

"Ah there now, you see?" Lord Campbell grinned with a sudden brightness to his voice. "Not everyone thinks that you have been tedious."

"I do hope that I have not interrupted your conversation, though I seem to be making a habit of doing so of late." Miss Millington smiled and accepted his arm when Adam offered it, and he smiled with pleasure when she did so. "You will be glad to know, however, that you have saved me from a prolonged conversation with my mother as regards two particular gentlemen my father intends to introduce me to."

At this, the light in her eyes diminished and her smile disappeared with it. Adam's heart twisted as he looked at her, seeing sorrow beginning to creep across her expression.

"We were doing very little other than talking about 'The London Ledger'," Lord Campbell remarked, clearly unaware of the changed expression on Miss Millington's features.

"'The London Ledger'?" she repeated, her eyes going wide. "I am surprised to hear that two gentlemen such as yourselves have read the Ledger."

"But we are members of the *ton* and, from what I understand, it is important reading! How are we to hear what has been taking place if we do not read so?"

Miss Millington laughed, her sorrow quickly forgotten.

"Indeed. And what was it precisely you were discussing?"

Adam's delight began to shatter as he shot a quick glance toward Lord Campbell, hoping that he would say nothing about the letter which Adam had confessed to, only some minutes ago. Much to his relief, Lord Campbell gave him a barely perceptible nod.

"Oh." Lord Campbell shrugged. "We spoke of a letter which had recently been placed within it, that is all." With a smile, Lord Campbell then quickly went on to change the subject. "But that was some time ago and now we wonder when news of Lady Margaret's wedding will reach us. It is to take place very soon, from what I understand."

Coughing quietly, Adam straightened, then smiled directly at the lady.

"Miss Millington, would you like to take a short turn around the park with me?"

Her hazel eyes instantly turned to gold as she smiled, only for it to fall away.

"I would like to accept but allow me to make certain that my mother will permit it."

With a nod, Adam watched as she stepped away, his eyes lingering on her. It was as if the sun had decided to shine a little brighter, now he was in her company. His heart was beating a little faster also, perhaps only just realizing how much he had missed her since the last time they had been in company together.

"Your thoughts linger on Miss Millington, I am sure of it." Lord Campbell tilted his head as Adam shot him a frown. "You need not look at me like that. I am quite certain that I am correct."

From experience, Adam knew that Lord Campbell's perception was usually correct, and seeing his friend grin, he shrugged and sighed.

"Yes, that is so. However, I..." Seeking something which would explain his strange interest in Miss Millington, which would explain how much his heart leaped when he saw her, Adam gave up entirely. After all, while he admitted to himself that such interest filled him, he had no clear thought as to what he might do about it. "She and I are merely acquaintances, that is all."

"And yet you do not wish me to say anything about the letter that you wrote to 'The London Ledger'." Lord Campbell folded his arms and chuckled. "There must be a reason that you wish me to hide that from her."

There was no simple explanation for that either. Lifting his shoulders in a shrug, Adam turned his head away, relieved when Miss Millington's approach made it impossible for him to explain himself. Lord Campbell's grin remained fixed, however, and try as he might, Adam could not ignore it.

"I am permitted."

With a broad smile, Adam offered her his arm again.

"Capital."

Her warm smile had his heart slamming hard against his chest.

"Thank you, Lord Seaton." Glancing away from him, she looked to Lord Campbell. "Are you to join us also, Lord Campbell?

"No, Lord Campbell is going to remain here and converse with your mother so that she is not alone."

Adam laughed aloud as Lord Campbell's delighted expression quickly faded to one of annoyance.

"Indeed?" Miss Millington's eyes flared. "Then I thank you, Lord Campbell, for your kindness. It is very good of you to be so willing. I am certain that she will appreciate the conversation."

"But of course." In the face of the obvious admiration and appreciation of Miss Millington, there was nothing for Lord Campbell to do other than what Adam had stated. "Do excuse me."

With what appeared to be gritted teeth and a low mutter of frustration sent in Adam's direction, Lord Campbell stepped away as Adam turned his attention again to Miss Millington. His smile blossomed as they walked arm in arm, and he was aware of a deep sense of contentment flooding him. Why he should feel such a thing simply from Miss Millington's company was inexplicable, but he was glad of it, nonetheless.

"You said something of your father a little earlier." Not wishing to pry, and yet at the same time rather interested to know what Lord Hayman had said to his daughter to make her appear almost sorrowful, Adam glanced at the lady only to catch the moment that her smile left her face. His stomach dropped. "Forgive me if I ought not to have asked."

"No, it is quite all right." Miss Millington let out a small sigh. "It is only that my father and I have very different expectations about my future."

"Oh?"

Again, she sighed and then glanced up at him, her eyes searching his for a moment, as though questioning whether or not she could trust him.

It seemed that she could.

"My elder sisters were given two Seasons each so that they might find themselves a suitable match. I, however, have not been given the opportunity and thus find myself deeply frustrated." Her lips pulled into a pout, her eyebrows lowering, and Adam's heart began to pound with a sudden unease. "They sought his guidance, of course, and the gentlemen who asked to court them had to be agreeable to my father, but they were not told *which* gentlemen to consider. They had the chance to make that choice for themselves. They were not subject to Father's demands in the same way that I am."

A swirl of breath tied itself into Adam's throat and, for a moment, he could not speak. When he did, his voice was low and rasping.

"Do you mean to say that your father is insisting upon you marrying?"

"It is the expectation that every young lady will find themselves a husband, is it not?" There was no lightness to her voice this time. "My father will be choosing my husband on my behalf, so he has said. That is the situation, as it stands. And attempting to speak with him, to request that he give me the same consideration as he gave my sisters, does very little." Adam blinked, trying to clear a sudden vision from his eyes, a vision of Miss Millington being forced to stand up in church alongside a gentleman she did not know, and certainly did not care for. It was as if someone had shot a bullet straight through him, such was the swell of pain at the thought. A little overcome by the swirling sensations, he looked away sharply. Why he should feel so strongly on her behalf, he could not quite understand but, all the same, his feelings lingered. Miss Millington continued, unaware of the feelings which had overtaken him, caught in her own unhappiness. "Perhaps I ought not to complain, however." Miss Millington continued, her tone a little lower now. "Mayhap many a young lady would be grateful for such a diligent father. It is only that I do not seek the same sort of match as he proposes."

"I do not understand what you mean."

What did she speak of? What was it that she wanted that her father was refusing to allow her? Surely it could not be that he was leaning towards someone who was a dear friend or long-familiar acquaintance as some gentlemen were inclined to do?

"I pray you will not think me foolish, for this has long been a desire of my heart." Again, she looked up at him, only to pull her eyes away, a soft pink on her cheeks. "I wish to marry a gentleman who will care for me. I do not want my marriage to be purely a practical arrangement, nor simply because of apparent suitability. Those things are distasteful to my mind, for I do not think that they lead to any sort of happiness." She took a breath, then continued, looking straight ahead rather than at him. "I have seen that my own parents, while they are good and kind in their own way, have not found any sort of happiness together. I hope that you do not think me rude or disrespectful to speak so, but it is only to show what sort of marriage I do not wish to have for myself."

"I do not think you so," he promised her, his words encouraging a small smile. "Sometimes we must speak as we feel, must we not?"

"Yes, I suppose so."

I must be careful in what I say.

The last thing he wanted was to make a fool of himself by speaking rashly but, at the same time, he wished to say something which would encourage her, which would offer her a sense of the esteem he held her in.

"I think you a very remarkable young lady, Miss Millington." As he spoke carefully, he saw her eyes light up again as her smile grew. "I am quite certain that you are *more* than able to make any great decisions for yourself."

"I could not agree more." Answering him with a quiet smile, she leaned into him a little. "Mayhap you ought to speak to my father about such a thing." The teasing in her voice made him laugh and, when he looked at her, her eyes were fixed on his, suddenly alive with obvious happiness. Around her face, a few gentle brown curls were being pushed this way and that by the breeze, although the rest of her hair was captured carefully by the bonnet. He could not help but sigh contentedly at the sense of sheer beauty which wrapped around Miss Millington and then flew over towards him, settling in his heart with a great warmth that did not leave him. He could not think of what to say, even though a good many things were on his mind for, whilst being in company with Miss Millington, he appeared quite unable to speak as clearly and distinctly as usual. "You are a gentleman willing to listen to me and for that, I am grateful."

Her quiet words helped to break the silence which had

captured him and, taking a deep breath, he pressed her hand with his.

"Would it be rather untoward of me to ask what it is precisely about these gentlemen whom your father suggests which displeases you so?"

Miss Millington did not immediately answer, her lips pursing as though she were deliberately choosing her words in her mind before speaking them aloud – and Adam grew a little anxious. Perhaps he ought not to have asked. It was only when she smiled and shook her head that he let out a slow breath, relieved that she was not about to berate him for such a question.

"Some time ago, there was a letter sent in response to another written in 'The London Ledger'." Suddenly she would not look at him and Adam caught himself frowning. "I know of what was contained within – and it was a harsh opinion against the urge to find a match which is *not* one of practicality or suitability."

Adam swallowed hard, aware that she was speaking of the letter which he himself had sent. Had one of her friends written the letter in the first place? Or had news of it simply traveled around society?

"How do you know of it?"

"My friends and I discuss many things, Lord Seaton." Finally, she glanced up at him, then looked away again. "I tell you this because my father is very much inclined to the same thinking as the author of that letter. He thinks only of practicality, rather than anything else. I am *not* a lady so inclined towards that, as I have said. I do not care about the connection one family will have to the next, nor do I care about whether my father thinks a gentleman wealthy enough. Those are not, to my mind, the things which might provide the grounding for a happy marriage."

Beginning to understand, Adam frowned and slowed their steps a little.

"What then is it that you do care about?"

"A gentleman's character." Miss Millington offered him a gentle smile, which he accepted with a clear understanding now flowing through his mind. "If a gentleman is cruel, then what good is a high title? If he cares only for himself, then what good is all the wealth he possesses? And if he has a dark temper, then what good is his well-connected family?" Her voice grew quiet as she spoke, her eyes looking away from him now. "What good is it to me if the gentleman I wed cares nothing for me?"

A little surprised, Adam turned and looked at her, coming to a stop.

"I am sure that most gentlemen come to care for the lady they wed."

"But in that regard, there is a chance that I might marry someone who would *never* come to have even the least bit of affection for me - and I do not want that."

Adam swallowed.

"You are seeking a love match."

His heart sank just a little as he looked into her face again and saw how her eyes warmed with a fervency that had not been there before. From what the lady had said, she wanted a love match – something he was quite set against, at least since his painful experience with Lady Margaret. And yet, he enjoyed Miss Millington's company immensely, found her delightful in conversation and, when at a ball, was always eager to have her dance with him. Why was it that her view on this particular matter caused his mind to turn over with uncertainty, his skin prickling as he looked down at her again?

"Yes, that is so."

"Then indeed, Miss Millington, I would advise you to put such thoughts from your mind. These things, I think, very rarely come to be. It is best to consider that someone your father offers you for practicality will not bring you the same difficulties that a *supposed* love match would! No, put such thoughts from your mind and consider sensibly, Miss Millington. You do not want to become a spinster, I am sure!" The same sentiments he had written in his letter came back to him in his words but, as he spoke, the smile vanished from Miss Millington's expression, and she looked away sharply. "I do not mean to speak harshly, but only to be as pragmatic as I think one ought to be."

Miss Millington's face went white.

"I think I should rather become a spinster than marry without love."

Her words were now a little sharp, her eyes flashing at him as she tugged her hand from his arm. With a lift of her chin, she held his gaze firmly and Adam's stomach dropped. He had never seen her in such a way as this before, suddenly appearing almost regal as though he ought to bow down before her and beg for her forgiveness.

I have spoken rashly. I have hurt her heart.

"I think I should like to return to my mother" Her lips pinched as she looked away. "I shall return at this very moment."

Adam swallowed hard, realizing now that Miss Millington no longer wished to be in his company.

"Miss Millington, I did not mean –"

"It is quite all right." Her tight smile was not enough to convince him. "It seems that you and I hold a very different opinion, and that is to be expected. I would not think that every gentleman in London would agree with me." Her eyes were shards of glass. "Thank you for our walk and conversation, Lord Seaton. Good afternoon."

There was nothing he could say to keep her by him, not even for a few moments more. He bade her farewell in a low voice and then watched her walk away, leaving behind a great chasm between them, one he did not think he would ever be able to close.

CHAPTER THIRTEEN

*O*h. *This is something of a surprise.*

"Might I offer you my hearty congratulations."

Lady Winterbrook sent an arched eyebrow towards Constance, who thankfully, due to the occasion was well able to smile, although she had to admit silently that she was also quite relieved. Lady Winterbrook, upon finding her at the ball this evening, had begged Constance to permit her to make the introductions to one Lord Rowney, the fourth gentleman who had written in response to Constance's letter and thus, it had been done. The gentleman was very handsome, just as Lady Yardley had stated, but was also very firmly betrothed.

"Indeed." Constance managed to add in. "How wonderful."

"I thank you," Lord Rowney replied with a grin. "It is only a recent betrothal, you understand, but I think we shall be very happy together."

"I am sure you shall." Lady Winterbrook murmured, smiling, and after a few more moments and expressions of delight, chose to step away, taking Constance with her.

"How unfortunate that we find that the gentleman is already betrothed!"

"You forget also that Lord Buckinghamshire is now courting Miss Macgregor," Constance reminded her with a sigh, for Lord Rowney had been the one to mention it during their discussion.

There was no smile upon her lips now, for that, unfortunately, meant that three out of the five gentlemen who had written to her were not in the least bit available for her to even consider. Lord Humphries was much too old. Lord Buckinghamshire was courting another and the third, Lord Rowney, was now betrothed. It seemed that she only had Lord Warrington from Scotland, and Lord Blayton – the one considered something of a dandy - to contemplate. Silently, she prayed that either one of them would be not only free from connection but also would also spark something within her.

"Have no fear, my dear friend. You will find what you desire, I am sure of it."

"I must hope that you are right."

Lady Winterbrook smiled in what was meant to be an encouraging manner, her eyes bright with obvious hope.

"Though there may also be someone *else* to consider."

"Who?"

Lady Winterbrook lifted an eyebrow.

"Why, Lord Seaton."

At this Constance immediately shook her head, her stomach dropping a little.

"No, my dear friend, I will not consider Lord Seaton."

"Whyever not?"

All of the emotion which had been building up within her threatened to overwhelm her as Constance's heart ached with a low, dull pain. It had been some three days since she had seen him in the Park, since they had last walked together and yet, even now, what he had said to her lingered in her heart. Up until that moment, she had not realized how much she felt for him. The truth was, her desire for his company had grown so great that she found herself close to utter despondency in realizing that he was not the gentleman she had thought him.

"My dear, you have become very pale." Lady Winterbrook stopped, turning directly and grasping Constance's hand. "Whatever has happened? I mentioned his name and suddenly, you seem sad."

Constance attempted to rearrange her features into a smile, but from the sharp look in Lady Winterbrook's eye, she knew that she could not pretend. Perhaps it was time to tell someone.

"I was walking with him some days ago. I cannot tell you how delighted I was to be in his company – and before you make any remark upon that, yes, I am aware that I have felt more for him than I allowed *myself* to previously admit. When he told me that he thought a marriage with love and affection was nothing more than a string of nonsense twined around one's heart, bringing hope with it before burning it up entirely, I found myself so heartbroken that I could barely speak."

Lady Winterbrook said nothing for some minutes, simply looking at her. When she did, it was with a heavy sigh.

"I have been observing you with Lord Seaton. I thought him very eager for your company, and I admit to being surprised when he did not seek to further your acquaintance."

"And because he has not, I have not permitted myself to feel anything." Constance struggled to keep her voice steady, aware of the tears which threatened, but caring very little as to whether or not they fell. To finally be able to speak of this, to admit it, not only to herself but to her friend, was a good deal more cathartic than she had expected. "I did not realize how much I wished for his prolonged company until I discovered how absent his heart would be from any connection we might make together."

"Oh, my dear." Lady Winterbrook squeezed her hand. "No doubt his stated opinion on this matter is because of his dealings with Lady Margaret."

Constance blinked.

"Lady Margaret?"

"Have you not heard?" Lady Winterbrook's eyes widened, only for her then quickly explain. "Of course, I forget that you are not inclined to listen to gossip at all. Let me tell you what I know - Lady Margaret has recently become betrothed."

"Yes, I am aware of that. "A slight frown pulled at her brow. "To the Marquess of Hadenshire, was it not?"

Taking a breath, Lady Winterbrook nodded.

"Yes. However, what you may not know is that Lord Seaton was first to declare himself to her." It was as if the air in Constance's lungs had frozen, a cold chill running over her skin, sending goosebumps prickling all over. A sudden memory came back to her - of her mother speaking with Lord Seaton, offering her sympathies for the disappointment Lord Seaton had recently encountered. She had quite forgotten it, seeing that Lord Seaton had not wanted to speak of it and she had chosen, therefore, not to question what her mother had meant. Was this, then, what her mother had spoken of? "I am sorry." Lady Winterbrook released her hand and then turned around so that they might look out at the ballroom together. "As I have said, his response now will come from her reaction to his declaration, for it has been said that she was not particularly kind to him with it. It may be that he does not *truly* believe that love and affection are foolish emotions, only that he has found himself so disappointed that he now desires to push all thought of such things away."

Blinking rapidly, Constance sniffed, accepting the handkerchief which Lady Winterbrook handed to her.

"If only I had not allowed my own heart to be so affected," she answered softly. "That is what has frustrated me so. How could it be that, upon hearing how little he thought of what I desire most of all, I only *then* realized how much I have come to care for him?"

Lady Winterbrook gave her a small smile.

"It is because the heart can do a great many things. It can hide our true self from us. It can hold onto anger and disappointment long after we think that we have forgiven and forgotten it. It can reveal the love we have for another before we have even had the opportunity to *think* of it."

"Then what am I to do?" She was a little frustrated with herself for she had managed to hide her emotions from everyone for the last few days, only for them now to pour out like a torrent. "How am I to rid myself of such feelings?"

"Alas." Lady Winterbrook lifted her shoulders, then let them fall with a sigh. "I do not think that you can." She offered Constance a small smile, as though that would be comfort. "That is the nature of love, I am afraid. It often comes upon you without your willingness, and certainly does not leave simply because you request it to depart. That is why it is said that one's heart can break on occasion. It may be because the love which one has is not returned by the other, and thus, one must bear the pain of unrequited love, while the love itself continues to linger on regardless."

Constance sniffed and turned away a little, wiping her eyes again.

"That is dreadful."

"Yes, I am afraid it can be." A quiet laugh came from Lady Winterbrook, but Constance knew it was not one of mirth. "Might I suggest...." She bit her lip only for Constance's eyebrows to raise in question. "Might I suggest that, if you are bold, you take yourself to speak with Lord Seaton about this?"

Horror thrust itself into Constance's heart.

"You think that I should tell him that I fear I am in love with him?"

"No, indeed, I did not mean that." Lady Winterbrook waved one hand. "Forgive me for my lack of clarity. No, what I mean to say is that you might speak with him about Lady Margaret. You could suggest that his heart is closed to all manner of things because of how his declaration to her was received. Perhaps it might aid you both."

Despite her friend's explanation, Constance could only feel a curl of disinclination.

"I do not think that I could."

Lady Winterbrook nodded in obvious understanding.

"Very well. Then might I say also, without meaning to be callous in any way, that you shall have to prepare your heart regardless. You have two other gentlemen whom you might consider, both of whom, according to their letters, seek a love match. Either that or your father will present you with someone very soon that neither your mother nor Lady Yardley will be able to protest about. Either way, my dear, you will soon be betrothed and you must prepare yourself for that. I know that you have long desired a match where your heart is filled with another and he is in love with you in return, but I must ask you if you can truly find a way to be contented if your marriage does not have love within it?" Constance closed her eyes, the thought so overwhelming that she found herself struggling even to accept it. "If you cannot," Lady Winterbrook continued, softly, "then pray, raise your courage, and speak openly with Lord Seaton in the hope that your words might ignite something within him. Perhaps then, my dear friend, you will gain what you have long hoped for."

Despite her friend's encouragements, Constance could feel nothing but despair in her spirit and, with fresh tears threatening, she shook her head.

"At this juncture, I find myself thinking that a gentleman whom my father considers appropriate may very well be the best choice."

Her voice was low, and her heart sank as Lady Winterbrook's eyes rounded in obvious surprise.

"My dear friend, you are speaking from a place of pain and disappointment which, while I understand, is not a good situation in which to make any sort of decision." Lady Winterbrook took her hand and patted it gently with the other. "Do not do anything until you have a chance to speak to Lady Yardley and the rest of your friends. We are all here to support you with this."

What was there to do but to agree? With only a minuscule nod, Constance lowered her gaze to the floor, her heart entirely unwilling to talk any further about what she now felt for Lord Seaton. What good would talking do? It would not lead to anything good.

"Thank you." Lady Winterbrook let go of her hand, sounding relieved. "I wish you did not have to feel such sorrow. I –"

"It now appears as though I am the one interrupting you."

Constance was not ready to lay eyes on Lord Seaton again, but he was in her presence regardless. A slightly strangled sound came from her throat as she fought to greet him, which was thankfully covered by Lady Winterbrook's effusive welcome.

"Lord Seaton." She smiled warmly as Constance quickly composed herself, taking a long, slow breath that lifted her shoulders and her chin. "We were at the end of our conversation, so you are quite welcome."

"I am glad to hear that." Lord Seaton smiled in obvious relief, but to Constance's eyes, it was not the same, warm, familiar smile he usually wore and, with his gaze dancing from one place to the next, Constance considered him a little uncertain. Perhaps he felt the same strain as she did at this moment. Her heart did not lift at this, nor give her any relief. Whatever he felt, she was sure that it could not be from sorrow and upset, as were the feelings which filled her own heart. Instead, it perhaps came from confusion and uncertainty, wondering why she was no longer as warm towards him as she had been some days ago. How could she be bold, as Lady Winterbrook had suggested? How could she speak to a gentleman who had very little understanding of what it was she felt – and who had been so quick to reject it as nonsense? "Are you dancing this evening, Miss Millington?"

Swallowing the knot in her throat, Constance tried to smile.

"I am not certain, my Lord." That was the truth for, thus far, no gentleman had come to enquire as to whether they might put their name on her dance card and, besides which, she was not in the best of spirits either. "My dance card is entirely empty as yet, so it remains to be seen whether or not I shall stand up with anyone."

"Mayhap if you did not hide your beauty in the shadows, then you would have many a gentleman coming to seek you out." His gentle words did not make her smile, although his compliment was appreciated, nonetheless. At seeing her lack of reaction, Lord Seaton's eyes suddenly flared. "Forgive me, I did not mean to insult you, or make to say that-"

"Do not worry, Lord Seaton." With a gentle laugh, Lady Winterbrook attempted to break the obvious tension. "We quite understand what you meant. Constance and I were seeking a place for a private conversation, which is why we stand here. I am sure that we are *more* than ready to return to the other guests."

Saying this, she turned her head and fixed Constance with a long look, making it quite clear to Constance precisely what was being asked of her. Would she be willing to put aside her hurt and disappointment and stand up with Lord Seaton again? Or was she too heartsore to do so?

The answer came quickly.

"I am afraid that I do not feel particularly inclined towards dancing this evening."

"Oh."

Her response immediately brought words of concern to Lord Seaton's lips, but she had no eagerness to hear them.

"I am quite well, I assure you, though fatigued by many thoughts and some disappointments."

It was as boldly as she could speak, as much as she dared reveal, and as he looked at her with widened eyes, she chose not to answer his silent questions.

Lord Seaton dropped his gaze from hers, a slow flush running up his neck and into his face.

"I see. Then I... I do hope that we will be able to dance again very soon."

Without another word, Lord Seaton turned away, moving back across the ballroom and away from them. As soon as he could not hear them, Lady Winterbrook turned to Constance, her eyes searching her expression.

"Are you alright? That must have been very difficult for you."

"I am *not* alright." Sniffing, she closed her eyes tightly, the heaviness of her heart pulling her so very low. "I do not think that I can stay here."

"Of course." Lady Winterbrook squeezed her hand lightly. "Would you like me to fetch your mother?"

Feeling tears approaching, Constance nodded. She had arrived at the ball with a determination to remain just as she was usually, to forget about the pain which had struck her ever since her conversation in the park with Lord Seaton – but now, all of her feelings had been brought to the fore. Now they had escaped from her, it seemed impossible to push them back into herself, impossible to contain.

She had no hope left.

∼

"Lady Winterbrook tells me that you are very upset over Lord Seaton."

Constance nodded but looked away.

"There is nothing to be done," she said softly, looking to Lady Winterbrook and giving a slight shrug of her shoulders. "You may explain all, Lady Winterbrook, if you wish. I do not have the words for it."

With a slight look of concern, Lady Winterbrook put a hand on Constance's shoulder, then told Lady Yardley all that had taken place. Constance looked away, her eyes still burning, quite certain that, should she speak, her courage would fail her, and tears would flow steadily down her cheeks. The ball continued all around them and the carriage would soon be ready to take Constance home but, in the interim, Lady Winterbrook had begged her to speak to Lady Yardley for only a few moments.

"I am sorry to hear that it has been so difficult." Lady Yardley put one hand on Constance's arm. "However, I would concur with Lady Winterbrook and encourage you to be bold."

"I do not think that I can."

Lady Yardley tipped her head.

"Might you write to him? It may very well be that, as has been suggested, he has been badly affected by Lady Margaret's response to his affection and thus, he now believes that all such emotions are frivolous and worthless. You could be the one to prove to him otherwise."

Constance shook her head.

"It would not surprise me, Lady Yardley, if he was the one who wrote that letter," she said softly, seeing Lady Yardley's eyes flare. "The words he spoke to me were precisely the same sentiments as were expressed within that letter. They were not exact in every way, but certainly the response was the same. I am quite certain that there is no hope for us. Therefore, with this knowledge, I must now consider what I am to do, for my father will soon find me another gentleman and, mayhap it would be wise for me to accept him."

"I could speak to the gentleman if you wished."

The softness of Lady Yardley's voice sent tears again to Constance's cheeks, but she dabbed them away quickly.

"I think that I have made my decision," she answered,

softly. "But I thank you for your kindness and for all that you have done."

Lady Yardley moved closer, her expression showing nothing but sympathy, but Constance turned away. The matter, to her mind, was at an end. She had no other choice but to go forward, knowing that she was separated from Lord Seaton, and would be forever.

CHAPTER FOURTEEN

"I do believe that this Season you have been more melancholy than I have ever seen you."

Adam snorted.

"Except I only came to London *last* Season," he reminded him, making his friend scowl.

"That is not what I meant. You and I have been friends for many a year. For whatever reason, you have gone from contentment, free from the shadows of Lady Margaret, only to plunge into an even *greater* darkness. You must tell me why. It is the only way to loosen your burden a little."

"Ah... I..."

"It is Miss Millington." Lord Campbell was the one to speak then, rather than allowing Adam any opportunity to answer the question himself. When Adam opened his mouth again to protest, Lord Campbell only chuckled. "Come now, do not fuss. I am correct, am I not?"

Adam shifted in his chair, wanting to shrug, wanting to refuse to say that yes, it was she who would not leave his thoughts but, aware he could not bring himself to lie, he said nothing.

"Why do you pretend that you do not care for her?" Lord Dennington stretched himself out in the sunshine, like an overly large cat, his feet stuck out in front of him, crossed at the ankle. "You find her delightful, do you not?"

Adam sighed loudly.

"If that is what you wish me to say, then I shall confess it. Yes, I find Miss Millington interesting and excellent company."

"And?"

Closing his eyes, Adam let out a hiss of breath between clenched teeth.

"And I cannot help but think of her. You will find this ridiculous I am sure, but that is the state of things."

"If you believe that we already are aware of your interest in the lady, then why do you wish to hide it from us?"

Adam flung up his hands, narrowly avoiding his drink on the edge of the table as he answered Lord Campbell's question.

"I cannot *allow* myself to feel anything for anyone! I have already had my heart broken by one young lady, and I believe now that any such affection is foolishness. It does not bring contentment or happiness. It fades quickly and burns up easily. That way lies only pain." Why was it that, as he said it, his heart no longer believed the words which his lips spoke, not now that Miss Millington had stepped away from him. He found himself suddenly desperate for her company and let his head drop forward. "It would be idiocy to allow myself to feel such things again."

This last sentence came out in a mumble, as his eyes squeezed closed.

"Surely you can see now that there is more to love than

what you felt for Lady Margaret?" Lord Dennington replied, calmly.

Adam hesitated.

"Perhaps."

"What you feel for Miss Millington, *that* is more like genuine affection," Lord Campbell interjected, "for not only is she someone worthy of your attentions, but I have no doubt that she returns them also." At this, Adam could say nothing, his mouth falling a little ajar as he looked back at Lord Campbell, silently thinking that he had offered the most ridiculous suggestion. Chuckling, Lord Campbell simply lifted both hands. "Come now, tell me that you have seen how she looks up at you? How her gaze lingers and how she smiles so brightly?"

Gathering himself a little, Adam frowned.

"She is behaving just as every other young lady does."

"I should disagree with you on that." Lord Dennington laughed as Adam's frown only grew. "You may not be thrilled with us saying such things, but that is the truth of it - and we tell you this for one reason only." The smile left his face as he leaned forward, his elbow on the table, one finger pointing towards Adam. "It is so that you not do not miss out on what so many other gentlemen seek."

"Which is?"

Folding his arms across his chest, Adam waited as Lord Dennington and Lord Campbell looked at each other.

"They seek love."

Lord Campbell spoke quietly but it was the slight catch in his voice that gave Adam pause. What they were both saying to him was not something he could simply ignore. Lord Campbell was speaking as a man who had found himself in such a position and had been gravely disappointed.

He lowered his head.

"If I admit to feeling anything for the lady then..."

Closing his eyes, he groaned aloud as both of his friends grinned, evidently delighted that they had broken his spirit enough for him to tell them precisely what it was that he was feeling.

Adam was not finding the experience pleasant.

"You believe it will injure you."

Nodding in answer to Lord Campbell's statement, Adam lifted his head and spread out his hands.

"I fear that it will be just as before. I have seen it repeated in the experiences of others. Therefore, I remain convinced that to have any feelings of affection or the like will, in the end, only bring sorrow."

"And why do you keep believing so?" Lord Campbell tipped his head. "Is it that you have witnessed my pain and seen my state of disillusionment and think it is the only representation of what happens when one's heart is involved?"

Pausing, Adam shrugged.

"Yes, but I think of myself also."

"But that was not love, as I have already told you." Clearly a little irritated, Lord Dennington rolled his eyes. "I understand that you believe that you fell in love with Lady Margaret, but I am quite convinced that you did not. Indeed, I think that you were only infatuated by her. I am not saying that you had no affection for the lady, only that it was not as deep as love is."

Adam frowned.

"For someone who has declared that they shall not wed either for practicality or for affection, you seem to know a great deal about matters of the heart."

It was a half-hearted attempt to take attention away from himself, but Lord Dennington only smiled.

"Or mayhap I have long been in love, and you have never known it," he said quietly. "Perhaps I wait for the young lady to take note of me."

"Which is yet another reason for me to push away all possible affection - for you may also find yourself disappointed," Adam shot back, but Lord Dennington held up both hands, shaking his head firmly.

"No, I am glad to feel such things and, even if I am to be disappointed, I shall be glad of it. To hold such a deep love within my heart has permitted me to see the world a little differently, to know what it is to care for someone beyond all sense. These are things I find myself grateful for, even though, for the moment, I must wait."

Lord Campbell cleared his throat.

"And it has proven to me that love is stronger than the pain I have suffered." Looking up from where his gaze had been resting on the table, Lord Campbell looked straight into Adam's face. "Yes, it is true that I have found myself battling a great deal of suffering. My heart has been sore and sick. I have hated the struggle and my heart's inability to remove Miss Barrett from my thoughts. However, I have learned that this has all been for a purpose." Adam caught his breath, his eyes rounding. "And yes, before you ask, I am finding my path forward with Miss Barrett."

Blinking, Adam's heart catapulted itself around in his chest and he could not give a single word of response. Part of him had been dreading this moment but, now that it was here, now that Lord Campbell seemed contented, he found himself strangely glad, glad that his friend would find a happiness that had been lacking from his life for so long.

"It will take some time to discuss, and there is much to share, but Miss Barrett has professed her heart to me, and I have shared mine with her. I did not like our separation, and I certainly did not like being pushed away, for the shame of it brought great suffering. I will not pretend that I was not injured because of it, but the truth now is, I love her enough to recover from all of these injuries. I hope to forget about them, to place them behind us so that we might step forward into what I hope will be a contented future." Chuckling, he shrugged both shoulders. "Certainly, I would have preferred *not* to have endured such pain, but the love within me, for her, has proven itself to be firm and long-standing. I do not doubt that it will carry me through for the rest of my days and I am grateful for it. I am overjoyed that my heart has found its way back to hers."

Taking a sip from his glass without really tasting it, Adam looked from one friend to the other.

"Then you mean to say that all that you felt, all that you endured, was worthwhile," he said, not quite certain whether he could take in such a truth, for it fought hard against what he had told himself to believe. "Therefore, you believe that I should admit to myself that my heart is full of Miss Millington, even though I have been determined to ignore it."

Lord Dennington nodded fervently.

"You certainly should."

"But even if I were to do so," Adam continued, speaking with great slowness, "I have already injured her most severely." The embarrassment which clawed at his heart begged him not to say anything more, but Adam spoke regardless. He told his friends of his conversation with Miss Millington in the park, of how he had mocked her desire for a love match and how she had, in return, stepped away from him. He told them of his request to dance with the lady, some days later, and how her refusal had brought him so much sorrow that it had made a misery of the rest of the evening.

"I see." Lord Campbell murmured, then smiled quietly. "What is it that you wish to do now?"

"I am certain that I can tell you." Lord Dennington tilted his head. "You will admit to yourself that you have done nothing but think of her and, thereafter, your mind will go to thoughts of how to make amends, eager now to have things between you as they were before." A satisfied smile crossed his face. "Is that not so?"

It was as if they had looked into his heart and told him of his own unspoken emotions.

"I confess, I do not even know what it is that I feel at present. I am all of a confusion, for I have been so very against allowing any emotion into my heart. It is difficult to permit it to fill with affection now. It is as though I am slowly breaking apart a dam, a little at a time."

"That is good." Lord Dennington grinned as Lord Campbell nodded. "You must tell her."

Adam shook his head.

"Even if I were to do so, it seems as though Lord Hayman is eager to secure a husband for his daughter. A husband of *his* choosing, I might add." To his surprise, neither of his friends appeared at all concerned. "You do realize what I am saying, do you not?"

Wondering how to explain himself, he blinked in surprise when Lord Campbell chuckled.

"I believe that both of us understand precisely what it is that you're saying, but we do not see the difficulty."

"How can you not?" Becoming a little exasperated Adam threw up both hands. "I have explained all to you. Lord Hayman is determined to find a suitable gentleman and -"

"And what makes you think that you are *not* a suitable gentleman?"

Adam stopped suddenly, his mouth closing with a snap. That was not something that he had considered.

"I... I do not have as much wealth as some. That is one of the reasons Lady Margaret rejected me." Speaking slowly, he let his thoughts run together quickly. "That may concern him; I may not have enough to satisfy him."

"I assure you, you have *more* than enough wealth to satisfy Viscount Hayman," Lord Campbell chuckled. "Lady Margaret was exceptionally greedy, and I am quite secure in saying Miss Millington is not so."

Nodding, Adam let his gaze fall to the floor, his heart thumping wildly at the prospect of speaking honestly to Miss Millington, and to her father.

"So you think that I should go and speak with him about his daughter?"

"Yes, but you ought to do so with caution." Lord Campbell held up both hands, one ticking off points on the other. "Firstly, you should inform him of your interest in his daughter. Then, you should make certain that all of your qualities are presented to him succinctly and, thereafter, you should make it plain what it is that you hope for. However," he continued, dropping his hands, "You should tell Miss Millington everything first. You must explain everything to her, for surely you want her approval before you approach her father?"

Keeping his gaze fixed on the floor, Adam said nothing. So many emotions were swirling around within him - shock, astonishment, confusion – that he could not sort one thought from the next. Was this truly how a deep affection felt? Was this what he desired? For if it was, then what exactly would he do to grasp hold of it?

"I need a little time." Rising from the table, he stuck out one hand to Lord Dennington and then to Lord Campbell, shaking both of their hands firmly. "I am aware that I have been something of a difficult sort this Season, but I am truly grateful for you both – for your long-suffering patience and your advice."

"We are glad that you listened to us!" Lord Dennington chuckled. "But all the same, I do hope that this will help you secure a genuine happiness."

Wincing, Adam shook his head.

"I am not certain that I deserve such things but, for the moment, I will take time to consider and then decide what I am to do next."

"Do not wait for too long," Lord Campbell warned. "From what I know of Lord Hayman, he is determined and quick to act. If he is firm in his intention to marry his daughter to a gentleman of his choosing, without delay – as you yourself have said – then he will already be acting upon it."

"And it does not sound as though she will have either a choice or the opportunity to offer a word of complaint to her father."

With a lift of his eyebrow, Lord Dennington's quiet urgency had Adam nodding solemnly.

"I understand. I promise you that it will not take too long."

Without another word, he turned and left, leaving his friends behind in White's, his mind filled with so many tangled thoughts that he could not separate them. Everything he had told himself, everything he had been quite certain of, was now thrown into confusion. If love was as strong as Lord Campbell stated, if it was as real as Lord Dennington believed, then he had been a fool to ignore it.

And Miss Millington had been the one to suffer for it.

CHAPTER FIFTEEN

There are only two gentlemen left.

Constance was all too aware of the fact that she had only two other gentlemen to meet out of the five who had responded to her letter. A heavy weight settled on her as she made her way to Hyde Park, alongside her mother and father – but strangely, it was not these two gentlemen her thoughts rested upon. Instead, she thought only of Lord Seaton and his reluctance to consider love as even the smallest possibility, and she painfully realized just how much distance there was now between them.

She missed his company, missed his smile, and the way that his eyes lit up whenever he glanced at her. She missed how her own heart quickened, how exhilaration had run through her whenever she had danced in his arms.

"It is the fashionable hour, Constance." Lord Hayman put a hand on her shoulder, catching her thoughts and throwing them away. "That means you must look your very best, which involves smiling."

Constance's breath hitched, her heart thundering at the understanding that her father was going to introduce her to another gentleman. Of course, she realized, this was why he had joined her and her mother in Hyde Park for the fashionable hour – there was a plan for her to meet someone.

"Who is it that I am to be introduced to, Father?"

His eyebrows lifted.

"I beg your pardon?"

"I understand now that you have joined us in Hyde Park so that you may introduce me to a gentleman who is under your consideration." Constance sighed heavily. "There is no need to pretend. What is this gentleman's name?"

"You have said nothing of the sort to me." Lady Hayman turned to her husband, her hands going to her hips. "You stated that you wished to attend so that we might go together, that was all."

"Which I did," Lord Hayman protested, though Lady Hayman did not seem to believe it. Her hands remained precisely where they were, her eyes flashing as she let out a low mutter of obvious disbelief. "Very well." Lord Hayman sighed, seemingly captured by his wife's demands. "If you must know, it is a gentleman by the name of Lord Warrington."

For some reason that name seemed familiar to Constance, and for a few moments she searched her memory, wondering whether or not they had already been introduced. She soon realized that they had not, but that this gentleman was one of those who had responded to her letter in 'The London Ledger'. She waited for a sudden thrill of excitement, for hope to lift her spirits, but nothing came. Instead, her heart remained heavy, her spirits low, and as she sighed, her mother immediately threw up her hands.

"You ought to be allowing Constance her own decision in this," she said sharply.

"And you and I have spoken of this already," came the hard response, although Lord Hayman kept his voice low. "There is no need to speak of it again."

"There is not, Mama." Constance put one hand on her mother's arm, managing a small smile. "And even if there was, this is certainly not the place to do it."

Lady Hayman shook her head, showing not the least bit of remorse at raising her voice.

"This has displeased me greatly, this whole affair. I am all the more ashamed that I did not realize the injustice of it before now."

"Be that as it may," Lord Hayman stated, his voice firm. "Lord Warrington is approaching us. Do turn, Constance, and smile."

Constance did only one of the things her father had asked of her - she turned but did not smile. She could not seem to force herself to do so, no matter the glances her father sent in her direction. Lord Hayman greeted the gentleman warmly, and Constance followed through the introductions carefully enough, curtseying when she was required to and thereafter letting her gaze settle upon Lord Warrington.

Much to her surprise, he was rather handsome, with dark brown hair which swept across his forehead. Sea-blue eyes, tinged with green, looked back at her as he offered her a quiet smile. When he spoke, his tone was soft, as though she were a gentle creature he did not want to scare away.

"Miss Millington. I am very pleased to make your acquaintance."

"As I am to make yours." Constance offered the

required response, having no genuine feeling behind those words. "Have you long been acquainted with my father?"

"It was my own dear father who was acquainted with Lord Hayman," came the reply. "I have been fortunate enough to continue the acquaintance."

Sighing inwardly, Constance nodded, but said nothing, assuming that her father was now going to speak of her to Lord Warrington as though she were not standing next to him, as he had done before, with other gentlemen. Instead, however, silence came upon the group. A little surprised, Constance looked up at her father, only to see him lift his eyebrow, his eyes swiveling towards Lord Warrington as though to ask her silently why she was not speaking.

She blinked.

"I - I hope that you have been enjoying the Season, Lord Warrington."

"I have a little." Lord Warrington lifted his shoulders, his hands now clasped behind his back. "As your father knows, I have recently taken on the title and, given that I take my responsibilities seriously, I will be blunt and state that I must marry soon and produce an heir. I hear that you, also, are seeking a match, Miss Millington. I have learned that you hope to find a match where affection is prominent. I can assure you, I hope for the same thing and, while I believe that affection might take some time to grow, I am sure that with intentionality, such a thing could be just as you desire."

Astonishment clouded her vision for a moment, and she caught herself staring. This was not at all what she had expected. Still astonished, she glanced at her mother, but she was not looking at her. Rather, she was gazing up at her own husband in clear surprise. What followed thereafter was a small smile, and Constance's own heart beat a little more quickly. It seemed as though her father had finally listened to either her own or Lady Hayman's protests, and had decided to alter his plans just a little.

Gratitude and relief poured into her.

"Might you wish to take a turn about the Park?" Lord Warrington gestured towards the growing crowd. "I am sure that we can stay within sight of both your fine parents."

Constance swallowed hard, still a little overwhelmed.

"Certainly, Lord Warrington. I should be glad to."

It would be rude to turn him down without any good reason and thus, with a brief smile to her mother and a glance at her father, Constance stepped away and took Lord Warrington's arm.

With a nod to Lord Hayman, Lord Warrington led her away from her parents and they began to walk together. Much to Constance's surprise, Lord Warrington had excellent conversation skills and, with his easy manner, it was simple enough to find herself contented in his company. He seemed amiable by first impression, was handsome enough certainly, with a warm smile and kind eyes. He spoke a little of his estate, of the fact that yes, it was *very* far away, but his description of it made it sound rather appealing. The more they spoke, the more at ease Constance became. Perhaps, she considered, this gentleman was the answer to all of her concerns.

But what of Lord Seaton?

The question ran around in her mind. She tried to shake it free, but it would not leave her. What about him? Could she so easily forget him? Forget the feelings for him which had built up within her? As much as he might have said that, no, love was not something he wanted to pursue, it was not something he thought had any viability, her feelings for him were lingering. Although she was sorrowful over the separation between them, her heart would not release him – even though she might desperately desire it to do so.

But I cannot tie myself to him.

Letting out a slow breath, Constance closed her eyes for just a moment. Yes, she might have to consider Lord Warrington, given that there could be nothing between herself and Lord Seaton. Perhaps in time there would be something between herself and Lord Warrington, something of significance, something she longed for - but for the moment, such emotions belonged solely to Lord Seaton.

"Your father tells me that you are not particularly enamored of his decision to choose a particular gentleman for you."

Heat boiled in the pit of her stomach, sending flames into her face.

"It is not that I am unwilling to hear his suggestions, Lord Warrington. It is only that I have no desire to betrothe myself to a gentleman I do not know, whose heart remains entirely hidden from me."

"Which I precisely understand." Lord Warrington smiled at her. "I believe that you and I are much of the same mind. I do not think that any real happiness can come from two people forced together for practicality's sake."

At this, Constance stopped immediately and twisted to look up at him.

"Is that so?"

"It is." He shrugged. "I have no doubt that you may believe that your father has told me to say such things, but I can assure you, I speak from my heart."

"I do trust you, Lord Warrington."

His green eyes warmed as he smiled.

"Indeed." He tilted his head. "You do not seem surprised."

For a moment, the answer came to her lips, ready to say that no, she was not surprised, for she already knew precisely the sort of match he was seeking, only to throw her response away. Certainly, she could not tell him that *she* had been the one to write the letter in 'The London Ledger' nor that she had read *his* response, seeking the same.

"I suppose that I have always believed that there will be some gentlemen within society who seek the same as I."

This answer seemed to satisfy him, for he nodded and smiled again.

"I am sure that there are more of us than it first appears." One shoulder lifted. "We do not all seek out wealth and beauty." At this, Constance's eyebrows lifted, and Lord Warrington immediately began to apologize, expressing that he did not mean to say that she was not beautiful, and Constance found herself laughing. With clear relief, Lord Warrington joined her in that laughter as they began to walk again. "If I have not made too much of a fool of myself, then I should like to spend a little more time with you, if I may." Lord Warrington looked down at her, his mouth pulling to one side just a little. "That is not to say that I intend to rush into courtship, however. If we both are eager for the same thing and have the same desires, then perhaps something may flourish between us but, if it does not, we can simply remain contented that we gave ourselves the opportunity."

He really was the most remarkable gentleman, Constance considered, and she was all the more glad that her father had behaved in such a way as to take what she had hoped for and bring it to the fore.

"I am not certain that my father will be so delighted if we decide that such a thing will not take place."

Lord Warrington chuckled.

"Be that as it may, he may have to suffer a little disappointment. I would not like to offer my heart if it was not returned."

She nodded and smiled at him.

"That is how I feel also. Thank you, Lord Warrington. You are most considerate."

"Miss Millington."

A voice broke between them and turning, Constance's heart slammed hard against her ribs. Lord Seaton was practically glaring at the Lord Warrington. He did not so much as glance at her, not even when she greeted him.

"Lord Seaton, good afternoon. Are you acquainted with Lord Warrington?"

Lord Seaton kept his gaze fixed.

"Yes. I am." Still without so much as looking at her, Lord Seaton narrowed his eyes just a little. "Good afternoon, Warrington."

"Good afternoon." Lord Warrington's pleasant tone was in complete contradiction to Lord Seaton's tight voice. "It is good to see you again, Seaton. I was sorry to hear about Lady Margaret."

"Pah!" The harsh exclamation made Constance's eyes round.

"You need not offer me any of your sympathies. In truth, I am glad of it, glad to realize that my feelings for the lady were not as I first believed them to be. I see now that I have been saved from what would have been the most disappointing marriage, and one which I would have come to regret, I am sure." Constance's eyes flared all the wider, but Lord Seaton had not finished.

"I confess that I thought myself in love with Lady Margaret, after only a few weeks of acquaintance. I realize now that these feelings did not have the strength which I first thought them to hold. Indeed, I see now that they were not as strong as love. It was something else entirely – an infatuation, nothing more." Slowly, and for the first time, his gaze turned towards Constance, as though he was speaking directly to her rather than to Lord Warrington. "Thereafter, I rejected all such feelings. I told myself that they were nothing more than foolishness, and I was determined not to permit myself any such sensations any longer. Even with my dear friend Lord Campbell, when I saw the struggle and the pain which he suffered over his own affection for a lady of quality, it made me all the more determined not to allow myself to feel anything. However, I was wrong."

A deep breath pulled at his chest. "Lord Campbell has taken your advice, Miss Millington, and he has found the beginnings of great happiness. The love he had for his young lady was enough to overcome the sorrows she left him with. The agony he battled for so long has begun to melt away and, I am quite certain, their bond will grow even stronger now."

She did not know what to say. What precisely was the meaning of all of this? Was it simply that he was speaking to her about Lord Campbell in the hope that she would see how much he appreciated what she had said? Or was there something more?

"I am afraid that I am not acquainted with Lord Campbell."

Lord Warrington cleared his throat, but Constance did not so much as glance at him. She was too delighted with all that Lord Seaton was saying.

Lord Seaton reached out one hand as if to take hers, only to drop it back to his side.

"This is all to say that my views on such things have altered significantly in only a few days." He lowered his gaze, his head falling forward just a little. "I am sorry, Miss Millington. I know that I was harsh, short in my response to you, and a little mocking in my words. I should like to ask you for your forgiveness, and to assure you that, as I have said, my perspective has changed drastically." When his head lifted, he found her gaze again. "I am glad that I have told you now, at least."

Upon saying this, he bowed to her, but did not so much as turn his head towards Lord Warrington, simply stepping away. Blinking rapidly, Constance fought to push aside the tears which immediately leaped into her eyes as he departed. Her heart was beating furiously, her mouth was dry, her mind twirling with a thousand thoughts as she fought to understand everything he had said. What did that mean for her? What did it mean for them? Was he, in his apology, attempting to reveal to her that there was something more in his heart for her, something he had never acknowledged before? And if there was, then what was it he now hoped for? Part of her wanted to run after him, to grasp his arm, to look into its eyes, and beg him to explain to her precisely what he meant by such things, and to ask if it could be as her heart so desperately hoped. Instead, she simply watched him walk away before finally returning her gaze to Lord Warrington, an apology on her lips for becoming so distracted.

"It seems I am not the only one considering a future with you."

Constance's eyes rounded.

"I did not know-"

"You need not fear. I will not stand in your path." Lord Warrington smiled and lifted his shoulders as she shook her head, protests dying on her lips. "But if you decide not to choose him, then you know that I will be willing to at least consider what the future might hold for us."

Nodding, with tears burning in her eyes, Constance could say nothing, a tightness in her throat stealing her voice. Lord Warrington, evidently on seeing this, smiled and offered her his arm.

"Come, let me return you to your mother," he said softly. "You have been away from them for some time already."

The only thing Constance could do was go with him, walking in silence as she kept her eyes fixed straight ahead, not taking a single thing in. Dare she allow herself to hope? And if she did, would Lord Seaton prove to her that he could bring the happiness which they might now both desire?

CHAPTER SIXTEEN

This is nothing but torment.

Setting his mind free from everything which had held him back meant that his emotions had exploded with such violence, he could not contain them. He could not tell himself to consider only one thing at a time, for his heart would not permit him to do so – but upon seeing Miss Millington walking arm in arm with Lord Warrington, dark clouds had thrust themselves upon him and he could not find a clear path.

"Drink this." Lord Campbell shoved a glass into his hand. "You say that you saw Miss Millington."

"Yes, with Lord Warrington." Adam's whole body shook with sudden frustration. "She was having the most pleasant time, it seemed, and then I decided to interrupt them."

Lord Dennington lifted his eyebrows.

"What did you say?"

Adam shrugged, his heart pulling low.

"I told her that I was sorry. And that I had been wrong." Running one hand over his face, not touching the brandy

Lord Campbell had given him, he let out a groan. "She is lost to me. Entirely."

"Why do you say so?" Lord Campbell shook his head. "You must be bold. She is not betrothed yet, they are not even courting."

"She may have accepted an offer of courtship, for all I know." A deep sense of despair filled him. "I discovered that Lord Hayman was the one to introduce them, which means that he considers Warrington a suitable match for his daughter. Lord Warrington is an amiable gentleman, for we all know him to be good-natured. In addition..." Trailing off, he felt a weight drop into his stomach, "he also seeks a love match."

At this, both Lord Campbell and Lord Dennington fell silent, and Adam's fears only grew.

"Before you ask, I have been aware of his desire for such a thing since last Season, for he spoke of it to me, and at the time I thought nothing of it. But now, to see him with Miss Millington fills me with grave concern, and a belief that I am much too late. She will find what she has long desired with him."

"Then, as I have said previously, you have no time to waste. I understand that you took only a few days to consider but can you not now see that you ought to have moved with a little more speed?"

"Berating me will do very little at this point." Adam shot a slightly dark look toward Lord Campbell. "Is there anything you think that I can do?"

Lord Campbell nodded slowly.

"First, consider. You may be over-exaggerating. It may not be as you fear. She may not have decided upon him."

"Though her father might have," Lord Dennington added with a grim look. "Forgive me for not being as positive as I ought to be, but that is my view of things. You must approach Lord Hayman before it is too late. I have no doubt that he will take very little convincing, given that you have a higher title and greater wealth than Lord Warrington - but it is not he whose approval you seek."

"No, it is not," Adam agreed quietly. "But how am I to convince *her*?"

The three friends sat together for some minutes in silence, each trying to think of a solution. When the idea suddenly came to him, Adam was on his feet in a moment, his heart in a sudden flurry of excitement.

"You have something." Lord Campbell grinned, suddenly delighted. "What is it?"

"It necessitates such haste, I have no time to tell you." Adam hurried to Lord Campbell's study door. "You will have to excuse me, I will tell you all very soon, I hope, but please do pray that I will be successful."

The two friends promised that they would do so, and with that, Adam left the room and hurried from Lord Campbell's house.

～

"I MUST ADMIT that this is something of a surprise."

"I am sure that it is."

After a bow, Adam walked further into Lady Yardley's drawing room and sat when she waved him to a seat. She gestured to the bell.

"Should you like me to call for some tea?"

"No, that will not be necessary. My visit will not be long." He looked at Lady Yardley, seeing her slightly widened eyes - but her gentle smile was enough to convince him that she was willing to listen, at least. He did not doubt that Miss Millington would have said something to her already, given how closely they were acquainted. "I am quite certain that I have injured Miss Millington a great deal." Speaking directly, he made his point clearly. "I have said some things to her which were rash and foolish, and I regret them all."

"I see." Lady Yardley did not shift in her expression but only nodded, though her eyes remained fixed on his. "I would have thought, Lord Seaton, that as you are aware of this, you would speak to Miss Millington herself rather than to me."

"And I can quite understand why you would think so." Taking a breath, he put out his hands. "However, I fear that she will not give me the opportunity to speak, given how sternly I threw back her idea of a love match. Therefore, I hoped to use 'The London Ledger'."

Lady Yardley's eyes rounded just a little.

"In what regard?"

Pausing, Adam licked his lips. What he was about to reveal was significant and would, no doubt, lower him in the eyes of Lady Yardley.

"Some time ago there was a letter within 'The London Ledger' from a young lady who sought a love match." Still uncomfortable, Adam got to his feet and began to pace slowly up and down the room, hoping that Lady Yardley would not mind his agitation. "I should like to use 'The London Ledger' to write a letter of my own. My intentions are-"

Lady Yardley held up one hand.

"Wait a moment, Lord Seaton. Do you mean to say that you do not know who the young lady was who wrote the letter?"

Pausing for a moment, Adam frowned then shook his

head.

"No, I do not. Miss Millington stated that she and her friends were merely discussing the letter, so she did not give me a hint as to who had written the original letter."

Lady Yardley paused for a moment, then sighed, her sharp gaze dropping away.

"I do not know whether I ought to keep this from you, or not, but I think it would be best you know. Lord Seaton, that letter was from none other than Miss Millington herself."

Adam could not breathe, the shock of what had been said was so overwhelming that it seemed to spread ice through every part of his frame. He stared at Lady Yardley, who nodded to confirm that what she was saying was true.

Heat burned through him, melting away the ice and he dropped his head into his hands.

"No."

His voice was hoarse and, as he lifted his head, Lady Yardley smiled sympathetically.

"I can understand your astonishment. However, I do not think that-"

"No, indeed, Lady Yardley, you do not understand." Throwing back his head, Adam ran one hand over his face once and then a second time. "I do not think that you understand at all. I have *truly* been foolish. Indeed, the significance of my actions is such that I would be surprised if Miss Millington should ever speak to me again." At her slight frown, Adam sighed again, then began his explanation. "The anonymous letter which Miss Millington spoke of, the harsh words written there..." His face burned and he closed his eyes. "It is not only Miss Millington who has written a letter, Lady Yardley." Opening his eyes, he gazed at her. "I wrote one in response."

On hearing her breath hitch, he nodded, then groaned aloud.

"You see then what I have done, Lady Yardley? She will not wish to even speak a word to me again after she discovers that *I* was the one who wrote that dismissive, abrupt letter to her!" Heaviness pushed him down into the floor, and he flung out one hand towards the door. "I shall take my leave, Lady Yardley. It seems as though all hope is lost."

"My dear Lord Seaton, do sit down again." Lady Yardley rose, smiling warmly, with one hand reaching out towards him, before gesturing for him to take his seat again. "It is not as bad as you think, I am sure of it."

"How can it not be?" Adam, unable to do as she asked me, continued to pace up and down the room. "I have ruined it. I have hurt her most severely, I am sure."

"But you are not that gentleman any longer." Lady Yardley's soft voice made Adam pause. "You do not hold the same feelings, I am sure."

"No, I do not." Speaking in a slightly hoarse voice, Adam slumped back down into his seat. "I am quite the opposite."

Tilting her head, Lady Yardley paused for a moment, then smiled.

"Am I to understand that you consider yourself in love with Miss Millington?"

There was not even a single moment of hesitation.

"Yes, yes, Lady Yardley I do."

"That is very good to hear." Lady Yardley drew in a long breath. "I cannot say more, for it is not my place to do so, but I do believe that you have every chance of regaining your acquaintance with Miss Millington."

His heart did not want to believe it, such was his shame.

"I do not know how you can say so." Adam hung his head, now hating every word that he had written. "Once she learns that it is I who wrote that letter - for I will not keep such a thing from her - I can already see the sadness in her eyes as she turns away from me."

After such a speech, there came a few moments of silence and thereafter Lady Yardley spoke in a gentle, calming voice, which urged him to answer.

"Tell me what you are doing here, Lord Seaton." Rising she went to ring the bell. "We shall take tea and discuss the entire matter. There is a reason you have come, a reason that you have not yet shared with me. You speak of 'The London Ledger', and writing a letter which you wish to have published." Her head tilted. "You may be surprised to learn that Miss Millington herself has not been particularly enamored of any of the gentlemen who, as yet, have written in response."

Adam shook his head.

"Though she may very well be now. Her father introduced her to Lord Warrington, and I know for certain that he seeks a love match. He made society aware of it only last Season."

The smile on Lady Yardley's face faded.

"You mean to say that her father has introduced her to him?"

Seeing the expression on her face, Adam nodded and closed his eyes.

"Yes, it is so."

"Then it is all the more urgent that we speak," Lady Yardley replied briskly. "Now do not hold back, Lord Seaton. Tell me everything, and tell me exactly what it is that you plan to do."

CHAPTER SEVENTEEN

"*A*nd what do you think of Lord Warrington?"

Her mother took Constance's arm as they walked together into the ballroom. Constance forced herself to answer, her mind having been entirely fixed upon Lord Seaton up until this present moment.

"He is amiable."

Her mother sighed contentedly.

"Yes, he is. For myself, I think that Lord Warrington is a gentleman of great worth, and I confess to having been *most* surprised to hear that he also seeks a love match. I knew that such a thing was important to you, but I did not think that your father would ever be willing to put such a gentleman before you. It seems that I may have misjudged him a little."

Constance managed a small smile.

"I would concur with that."

"Mayhap Lord Warrington will be here this evening, and you will be able to dance with him!"

With a small sigh, Constance forced her lips to pull into a smile. She was not in the least bit enamored of the idea of being at a ball, but society dictated that she attend since the invitation had already been accepted. It would be poor form not to do so, and it was not as though she could hide away. Nor could she explain to her mother that she was heartsick over a gentleman who did not have any intention of falling in love. How could she tell her that the only gentleman who now filled her heart was not someone she could ever contemplate marrying, given that he would never permit himself to fall in love?

"If you do not think Lord Warrington suitable, I am certain that your father will find another." This was said without any threat, only as an acknowledgment of the truth. "I do think that he will be a little more careful with his suggestions from now on."

Constance looked at her mother.

"That is good, at least, although I am sure that father hopes desperately for my affections to fall upon Lord Warrington."

Lady Hayman nodded.

"I am certain that is true, my dear, but my own considerations are not the same as your father's. After all," she continued with a slight catch to her voice, "Scotland is so *very* far away."

Sudden tears burned, and Constance said nothing, falling into step with her mother as they made their way into the ballroom, her arm tightening just a little. It was only when Lady Yardley waved to her that Constance excused herself and her mother let her go, seeing now that she was to speak to her friend.

❧

"Good evening, Lady Yardley ."

The lady smiled just as Lady Winterbrook joined them.

"Good evening. I am very glad to see you this evening."

For whatever reason, there was a brightness in Lady Yardley's voice that Constance had not expected. Perhaps, she considered, Lady Yardley was doing her best to lift Constance's spirits.

"Another ball." Lady Winterbrook smiled. "I know that Lord Warrington is to be present, and I hear you have been enjoying his company of late."

Constance shook her head.

"I have walked with him once, and he came to take tea the day after. That is all."

"And do you find him a pleasant gentleman?"

Constance could not help but sigh.

"Yes, of course, but you know very well that I cannot think of him in any other way than as an acquaintance. A kind person, certainly, but not one whom I could give my heart to. However," she continued with a sad smile, "I have resigned myself to the fact I have no other choice but to marry a gentleman I do not particularly care for. My hopes for a marriage of love are quite gone from me."

"Because of Lord Seaton?"

Lady Yardley smiled, then took Constance's hand.

"My dear, there is something I wish you to read."

Constance frowned.

"To read?" she repeated as Lady Yardley nodded.

"Yes. It is a copy of 'The London Ledger' which was only published earlier this evening," Lady Yardley replied. "I have made certain that those at the ball are amongst the first to receive a copy. Should you like to peruse it?"

From the look in Lady Yardley's eye, it was obvious that there was something within the Ledger that Constance was meant to see. Without a word, she took the copy which was handed to her by Lady Yardley but did not look down at it.

Instead, she searched her friend's face, wondering why there seemed to be such a spark in her eyes. Was it that another gentleman had decided to write a letter in response to hers – even though it was some time ago - eagerly expressing his hopes for love and affection within it? Was she to be given another hope in that regard?

Do they not understand? I can love no other but Lord Seaton, even though he will never return my affections.

"Please, do read it."

Now it was Lady Winterbrook's turn to encourage her, giving her a warm smile before gesturing to the Ledger. Constance glanced around the room. There were some people already reading 'The London Ledger'. Some were using it to fan themselves, whilst others were pointing at different parts, heads close to one another as they perused it. With another frown directed towards Lady Yardley, she finally turned her gaze down to it, her eyes going to the part Lady Yardley pointed out.

It was a letter. Slowly, Constance began to read, her heart filling with growing astonishment as she took in each word.

'I should like to declare to all who read this that I am nothing short of a fool. I am a gentleman who has had cause to be injured by the words of another and therefore I set my entire mind and heart against all affection and love. Indeed, I even went so far as to write a letter to the young lady who searched desperately for a gentleman of the same desires as she: a marriage where love and affection grew strong together. I wrote harsh, cruel words which were undeserved, speaking from the pain and upset of my heart. It was foolish to do so, and I wrote those lines without pausing even to think. I admit to all of London society who will read this letter and see the words which I write here, that it showed great

stupidity and lack of consideration on my part. I do so without hesitation, for I know that I have injured one particular young lady by my words, and it is to her that this letter is written.

I confess to you not only that I was the gentleman who wrote such harsh words, but that I was also the gentleman who found himself drawn to you but refused to allow his heart to admit it. I hurt you when I laughed at your earnest desires. I told you that love and affection were not attributes anyone ought to seek, given how little joy or happiness they brought. I remarked that anyone who permitted such a thing into their heart, knowing the pain it might then cause them, was nothing short of foolish. My dear lady, I admit openly now that I was wrong. It was only my pain that spoke, and I used that emotion to hide from myself the truth of my heart. I will admit that truth to you now. I will confess that I have fallen in love with you and that my only desire is to forever be in your company. I should never have said what I did as we walked together in the park, I should never have written that letter with those remarks, and I only pray that you might find it within yourself to forgive me. The realization that you might now be chosen by someone else has torn my heart, flesh, and bone asunder. I care for you. The only desire of my heart is for you. I pray that you have not been stolen away by another as yet, for I will do whatever I must to place myself back into your heart again. If I am to have your sweetness, if I am to be blessed with your company once more, then I shall forever be grateful. Look upon me as a fool, if you must, for that is what I am, but pray turn your sweet eyes upon me again. Consider whether you might be willing to forgive my idiocy, knowing that you have a gentleman who now realizes how much he cares for you. It is my fervent hope that you feel a little of *the same, for then, mayhap, we shall both find what we have been praying for.'*

Constance read all of this with a pounding heart, her mouth a little ajar as her eyes struggled to take it all in.

Lord Seaton?

Was it that the gentleman who had written this letter was also the one who had sent her such a cruel response to her original letter in the 'London Ledger'? Surely it could not be! Her hand fell to her side as she lifted her head, looking straight at Lady Yardley.

"I cannot quite believe this."

Lady Yardley smiled and squeezed her hand and, as Constance's vision blurred again, she looked over the letter and took in the name written there as if to confirm it to herself.

Lord Seaton.

"He is waiting for you, my dear." A gentle hand on Constance's shoulder directed her across the ballroom. "He waits to see your response. I would urge you to go to him. Only do as you wish." Her eyes softened. "What does your heart say?"

Constance did not give a single word of reply. Instead, she simply handed the Ledger back to Lady Yardley and, without so much as a glance at Lady Winterbrook, made her way directly across the ballroom to Lord Seaton. She had to weave in and out of the crowd, but kept her eyes fixed on him, her heart so furious in its beating, it was the only thing that she could hear. Lord Seaton was looking at her but, as she drew closer, his eyes dropped, and when he came fully into her view, she saw the uncertainty of his stance. He was shifting from one foot to the other, his hands clasping tightly in front of him and then loosening again. Swirling blue eyes looked up at her, then dropped away again, as if he were preparing himself for whatever it was that she was going to say.

"You wrote this letter, in the Ledger today."

Constance's voice was thick with tears, but she held them back with an effort. Finally, Lord Seaton looked directly at her, his eyes locking upon hers.

"Yes. I did. It was the only thing I could think to do, the only way to express my regret and confess the truth of my heart. It was the only way I could be sure that you would hear it all from me."

Breathing rapidly, Constance attempted to steady herself.

"And you meant every word?

"As though it were written with every beat of my heart." Taking a step closer, he put one hand out to her. "I have realized, too late, how much I care for you. I took too long to understand what I was searching for. I held myself back for too long before I searched my heart and realized the truth. But that is my confession, Miss Millington, and yes, every word is honest and true. I have held nothing back."

Biting her lip, Constance lifted her chin just a little, her heart overflowing. All was suddenly wonderful and beautiful and there was no darkness or shadow any longer.

"It is not too late, Lord Seaton," she told him, watching his eyes round just a little. "It is not too late at all."

EPILOGUE

*a*dam could do nothing but stare at her. Was that truly what she had said, or had his ears chosen to deceive him, giving him hope he did not deserve? It was only when she laughed and looked away, her cheeks filled with color, he realized that, firstly, he had not responded to her and secondly, that yes, he *had* heard her correctly. Swallowing hard, he dropped his head and closed his eyes tightly, one hand curling close into a fist to contain the swell of emotions that threatened to overpower him.

"Lord Seaton?"

Lifting his head, he looked back into her wide eyes.

"I can hardly believe the happiness I feel at this moment," he said by way of reassurance. "It is more than I deserve. I must have hurt you so grievously and yet-"

"Let us not speak of that now."

When his hand uncurled from the tight fist which he had held it in, Miss Millington moved closer and reached out, her fingers running over his for just a moment – only to jerk her hand back and glance around the room for fear that someone would see them.

How much I want to be close to her at this moment.

Throwing all caution aside, he looked to his left, then, catching her eye, tilted his head in the direction of the open door and moved towards it. Miss Millington, much to his relief, followed him after some minutes and, thereafter, moved past him into a small, quiet room that hid them from prying eyes. It was most improper, of course, but they would only be gone for a few moments, he told himself. He had to have at least one moment alone with her.

Adam stood with his back through the door so that no one would be easily able to enter. Silence washed through the room and, his throat constricting, he suddenly did not know what to say. His gaze held hers steadily, the gentle smile on her face lighting her eyes.

"I will not be presumptuous." His voice was a little hoarse, and he smiled softly at her. "I will not do anything which we ought not to do, for I want now to confess to you openly that my heart belongs to you, Miss Millington. I did not see it for so long. I rejected the feeling entirely and, in doing so, hurt you grievously. I am sorry for all of my foolishness, for that is what it was. I injured myself also, however, by refusing to permit my heart to be free to love. Now that I have allowed myself to feel all that I do, I am aware of just how great my love and affection is for you. To that end, Miss Millington, I confess that the only desire I have at present is to court you."

"That is just what – oh!" One hand flew to her mouth, her eyes rounding. "I was to tell you such a desire is all that is in my own heart also, only to remember that my father is quite determined that *he* will find a suitable gentleman for me. He has already placed one fellow in front of me – Lord Warrington – and I–"

Before she could continue, Adam had stepped forward

and caught her hand, silencing her. Her fingers were soft, and he laced his through hers, tying them together.

"I have already spoken to your father." This explanation made her eyes round all the more, and Adam laughed a little ruefully. "I wanted to make certain that such a decision was your own entirely. Thus, I went to speak to your father in the hope that he might agree that, if you were willing to court me, I should already have his permission also. Much to my relief, he consented." Miss Millington did not seem to know how to respond, for her mouth fell open, only for it to close again as her eyes flooded with tears. She blinked them away, rapidly shaking her head, and Adam suddenly feared that he had done something wrong. Perhaps he ought to have confessed himself to her first before speaking to Lord Hayman, but he had wanted very much to make certain that he had the gentleman's permission so that Miss Millington had nothing but free choice before her. "I am sorry if I did not do what was right in your eyes."

"Oh no, Lord Seaton." Miss Millington's voice was soft, breaking gently, but her eyes were fixed on his, a gentle smile upon her lips as she finally turned her head back towards him. "It is only that I am astounded, overcome with delight, wonder, hope, and joy. For so long I have desired this and, when my father first gave me his edict, I confess that I lost a great deal of hope. It has all come to fruition, however, and as I stand here with you, our hands together, I realize the beautiful gift which I have been given - something I thought I should never have, something I thought had already been taken from me. Yet look how love has found its way forward."

"Yes, it has." Adam took a step closer to her, wanting desperately to kiss her, wanting to prove his love to her through such a gesture, but holding himself back firmly. He would not push her into something she did not desire. "I have said to you that I love you, Miss Millington – Constance - and that is all my heart feels. It is a torrent within my heart, flooding through every part of me, and that fountain will never be stopped. Indeed, I am certain that it will only grow stronger. In the time that we spend together, I shall find you all the more beautiful, all the more wonderful, all the more remarkable."

"Your compliments are delightful, but your words of love are even sweeter." Her free hand settled against his heart, and it roared immediately into greater life, pounding furiously against his chest. "It seems as though we have found our way together, our hearts already filled with the love neither of us immediately understood. But now that I see the truth of it, now that I can speak freely of all I desire, I will tell you, Lord Seaton, that my heart will always be yours. I love you desperately, to the point that it has pained me with nothing but tears and sorrow, believing that we should always be separated and that I should never have the chance to love you in the way that I wish."

"But that is what you have now," he promised her, softly. "Once we have courted for a time, my sole intention is to propose, and I hope that you will say yes when the time comes."

Laughing, she smiled at him.

"I shall say yes at this moment!" she retorted with a toss of her head, her eyes bright with love. "I shall be yours and you shall be mine, for I love you with all of my heart."

"As I love you."

He lowered his head, and she was waiting for him. Their lips met for the briefest of kisses, but it was enough to satisfy the desperate longing within his soul. His arms wrapped around her waist, and he held her close, her head going to his shoulder. Adam closed his eyes, a soft smile curling around his lips. Love had found him and with it, a happiness which nothing else could ever offer him. Their love would grow with every day that they spent together, their bond forging ever stronger so that they remained forever as one.

He could think of no better future than that.

Oh my! This is the last book in this series!

Did you miss the first book in the **Only for Love** series? The Heart of a Gentleman Read ahead for a sneak peek!

Christmas is coming! And to celebrate I am releasing a box set of my Christmas house party stories. Check it out in the Kindle store! Christmas Kisses Box Set

MY DEAR READER

Thank you for reading and supporting my books! I hope this story brought you some escape from the real world into the always captivating Regency world. A good story, especially one with a happy ending, just brightens your day and makes you feel good! If you enjoyed the book, would you leave a review on Amazon? Reviews are always appreciated.

Below is a complete list of all my books! Why not click and see if one of them can keep you entertained for a few hours?

The Duke's Daughters Series
The Duke's Daughters: A Sweet Regency Romance Boxset
A Rogue for a Lady
My Restless Earl
Rescued by an Earl
In the Arms of an Earl
The Reluctant Marquess (Prequel)

A Smithfield Market Regency Romance
The Smithfield Market Romances: A Sweet Regency Romance Boxset
The Rogue's Flower
Saved by the Scoundrel
Mending the Duke
The Baron's Malady

The Returned Lords of Grosvenor Square
The Returned Lords of Grosvenor Square: A Regency
Romance Boxset
The Waiting Bride
The Long Return
The Duke's Saving Grace
A New Home for the Duke

The Spinsters Guild
The Spinsters Guild: A Sweet Regency Romance Boxset
A New Beginning
The Disgraced Bride
A Gentleman's Revenge
A Foolish Wager
A Lord Undone

Convenient Arrangements
Convenient Arrangements: A Regency Romance
Collection
A Broken Betrothal
In Search of Love
Wed in Disgrace
Betrayal and Lies
A Past to Forget
Engaged to a Friend

Landon House
Landon House: A Regency Romance Boxset
Mistaken for a Rake
A Selfish Heart
A Love Unbroken
A Christmas Match
A Most Suitable Bride

An Expectation of Love

Second Chance Regency Romance
Second Chance Regency Romance Boxset
Loving the Scarred Soldier
Second Chance for Love
A Family of her Own
A Spinster No More

Soldiers and Sweethearts
To Trust a Viscount
Whispers of the Heart
Dare to Love a Marquess
Healing the Earl
A Lady's Brave Heart

Ladies on their Own: Governesses and Companions
Ladies on their Own Boxset
More Than a Companion
The Hidden Governess
The Companion and the Earl
More than a Governess
Protected by the Companion

Lost Fortunes, Found Love
A Viscount's Stolen Fortune
For Richer, For Poorer
Her Heart's Choice
A Dreadful Secret
Their Forgotten Love
His Convenient Match

Only for Love

The Heart of a Gentleman
A Lord or a Liar
The Earl's Unspoken Love
The Viscount's Unlikely Ally
The Highwayman's Hidden Heart
Miss Millington's Unexpected Suitor

Christmas Stories
Love and Christmas Wishes: Three Regency Romance
Novellas
A Family for Christmas
Mistletoe Magic: A Regency Romance
Heart, Homes & Holidays: A Sweet Romance Anthology

Christmas Kisses Series
Christmas Kisses Box Set
The Lady's Christmas Kiss
The Viscount's Christmas Queen
Her Christmas Duke

Happy Reading!
All my love,
Rose

A SNEAK PEEK OF THE
HEART OF A GENTLEMAN

CHAPTER ONE

"Thank you again for sponsoring me through this Season." Lady Cassandra Chilton pressed her hands together tightly, a delighted smile spreading across her features as excitement quickened her heart. Having spent a few years in London, with the rest of her family, it was now finally her turn to come out into society. "I would not have been able to come to London had you not been so generous."

Norah, Lady Yardley smiled softly and slipped her arm through Cassandra's.

"I am just as glad as you to have you here, cousin." A small sigh slipped from her, and her expression was gentle. "It does not seem so long ago that I was here myself, to make my Come Out."

Cassandra's happiness faded just a little

"Your first marriage was not of great length, I recall." Pressing her lips together immediately, she winced, dropping her head, hugely embarrassed by her own forthrightness "Forgive me. I ought not to be speaking of such things."

Thankfully, Lady Yardley chuckled.

"You need not be so concerned, my dear. You are right to say that my first marriage was not of long duration, but I *have* found a great happiness since then - more than that, in fact. I have found a love which has brought me such wondrous contentment that I do not think I should ever have been able to live without it." At this, Cassandra found herself sighing softly, her eyes roving around the London streets as though they might land on the very gentleman who would thereafter bring her the same love, within her own heart, that her cousin spoke of. "But you must be cautious," her cousin continued. "There are many gentlemen in London – even more during the Season – and not *all* of them will seek the same sort of love match as you. Therefore, you must always be cautious, my dear."

A little surprised at this, Cassandra looked at her cousin as they walked along the London streets.

"I must be cautious?"

Her cousin nodded sagely.

"Yes, most careful, my dear. Society is not always as it appears. It can be a fickle friend." Lady Yardley glanced at Cassandra then quickly smiled - a smile which Cassandra did not immediately believe. "Pray, do not allow me to concern you, not when you have only just arrived in London!" She shook her head and let out an exasperated sigh, evidently directed towards herself. "No doubt you will have a wonderful Season. With so much to see and to enjoy, I am certain that these months will be delightful."

Cassandra allowed herself a small smile, her shoulders relaxing in gentle relief. She had always assumed that London society would be warm and welcoming and, whilst there was always the danger of scandal, that danger came only from young ladies or gentlemen choosing to behave improperly. Given that she was quite determined *not* to behave so, there could be no danger of scandal for her!

"I assure you, Norah, that I shall be impeccable in my behavior and in my speech. You need not concern yourself over that."

Lady Yardley touched her hand for a moment.

"I am sure that you shall. I have never once considered otherwise." She offered a quick smile. "But you will also learn a great deal about society and the gentlemen within it – and that will stand you in good stead."

Still not entirely certain, and pondering what her cousin meant, Cassandra found her thoughts turned in an entirely new direction when she saw someone she recognized. Miss Bridget Wynch was accompanied by another young lady who Cassandra knew, and with a slight squeal of excitement, she made to rush towards them – somehow managing to drag Lady Yardley with her. When Cassandra turned to apologize, her cousin laughingly disentangled herself and then urged Cassandra to continue to her friends. Cassandra did so without hesitation and, despite the fact it was in the middle of London, the three young ladies embraced each other openly, their voices high with excitement. Over the last few years, they had come to know each other as they had accompanied various elder siblings to London, alongside their parents. Now it was to be their turn and the joy of that made Cassandra's heart sing.

"You are here then, Cassandra." Lady Almeria grasped her hand tightly. "And you were so concerned that your father would not permit you to come."

"It was not that he was unwilling to permit me to attend, rather that he was concerned that he would be on the continent at the time," Cassandra explained. "In that regard, he was correct, for both my father *and* my mother have taken leave of England, and have gone to my father's properties on the continent. I am here, however, and stay now with my cousin." Turning, she gestured to Lady Yardley who was standing only a short distance away, a warm smile on her face. She did not move forward, as though she was unwilling to interrupt the conversation and, with a smile of gratitude, Cassandra turned back to her friends. "We are to make our first appearances in Society tomorrow." Stating this, she let out a slow breath. "How do you each feel?"

With a slight squeal, Miss Wynch closed her eyes and shuddered.

"Yes, we are, and I confess that I am quite terrified." Taking a breath, she pressed one hand to her heart. "I am very afraid that I will make a fool of myself in some way."

"As am I," Lady Almeria agreed. "I am afraid that I shall trip over my gown and fall face first in front of the most important people of the *ton*! Then what shall be said of me?"

"They will say that you may not be the most elegant young lady to dance with?" Cassandra suggested, as her friends giggled. "However, I am quite sure that you will have a great deal of poise – as you always do – and will be able to control your nerves quite easily. You will not so much as stumble."

"I thank you for your faith in me."

Lady Almeria let out a slow breath.

"Our other friends will be present also," Miss Wynch added. "How good it will be to see them again – both at our presentation and at the ball in the evening!"

Cassandra smiled at the thought of the ball, her stomach twisting gently with a touch of nervousness.

"I admit to being excited about our first ball also. I do

wonder which gentlemen we shall dance with." Lady Almeria swiveled her head around, looking at the many passersby before leaning forward a little more and dropping her voice low. "I am hopeful that one or two may become of significant interest to us."

Cassandra's smile fell.

"My cousin has warned me to be cautious when it comes to the gentlemen of London." Still a little disconcerted by what Lady Yardley had said to her, Cassandra gave her friends a small shrug. "I do not understand precisely what she meant, but there is something about the gentlemen of London of which we must be careful. My cousin has not explained to me precisely what that is as yet, but states that there is much I must learn. I confess to you, since we have all been in London before, for previous Seasons – albeit not for ourselves – I did not think that there would be a great deal for me to understand."

"I do not know what things Lady Yardley speaks of," Miss Wynch agreed, a small frown between her eyebrows now. "My elder sister did not have any difficulty with *her* husband. When they met, they were so delighted with each other they were wed within six weeks."

"I confess I know very little about Catherine's engagement and marriage," Lady Almeria replied, speaking of her elder sister who was some ten years her senior. "But I *do* know that Amanda had a little trouble, although I believe that came from the realization that she had to choose which gentleman was to be her suitor. She had *three* gentlemen eager to court her – all deserving gentlemen too – and therefore, she had some trouble in deciding who was best suited."

Cassandra frowned, her nose wrinkling.

"I could not say anything about my brother's marriage, but my sister did wait until her second Season before she accepted a gentleman's offer of courtship. She spoke very little to me of any difficulties, however - and therefore, I do not understand what my cousin means." A small sigh escaped her. "I do wish that my sister and I had been a little closer. She might have spoken to me of whatever difficulties she faced, whether they were large or small, but in truth, she said very little to me. Had she done so, then I might be already aware of whatever it is that Lady Yardley wishes to convey."

Miss Wynch put one hand on her arm.

"I am sure that we shall find out soon enough." She shrugged. "I do not think that you need to worry about it either, given that we have more than enough to think about! Maybe after our come out, Lady Yardley will tell you all."

Cassandra took a deep breath and let herself smile as the tension flooded out of her.

"Yes, you are right." Throwing a quick glance back towards her cousin, who was still standing nearby, she spread both hands. "Regardless of what is said, I am still determined to marry for love."

"As am I." Lady Almeria's lips tipped into a soft smile. "In fact, I think that all of us – our absent friends included – are determined to marry for love. Did we not all say so last Season, as we watched our sisters and brothers make their matches? I find myself just as resolved today as I was then. I do not think our desires a foolish endeavor."

Cassandra shook her head.

"Nor do I, although my brother would have a different opinion, given that he trumpeted how excellent a match he made with his new bride."

With a wry laugh, she tilted her head, and looked from one friend to the other.

"And my sister would have laughed at us for such a

suggestion, I confess," Lady Almeria agreed. "She states practicality to be the very best of situations, but I confess I dream of more."

"As do I." A slightly wistful expression came over Miss Wynch as she clasped both hands to her heart, her eyes closing for a moment. "I wish to know that a gentleman's heart is filled only with myself, rather than looking at me as though I am some acquisition suitable for his household."

Such a description made Cassandra shudder as she nodded fervently. To be chosen by a gentleman simply due to her father's title, or for her dowry, would be most displeasing. To Cassandra's mind, it would not bring any great happiness.

"Then I have a proposal." Cassandra held out her hands, one to each of her friends. "What say you we promise each other – here and now, that we shall *only* marry for love and shall support each other in our promises to do so? We can speak to our other friends and seek their agreement also."

Catching her breath, Lady Almeria nodded fervently, her smile spreading across her face.

"It sounds like a wonderful idea."

"I quite agree." Miss Wynch smiled back at her, reaching to grasp Cassandra's hand. "We shall speak to the others soon, I presume?"

"Yes, of course. We shall have a merry little band together and, in time, we are certain to have success." Cassandra sighed contentedly, the last flurries of tension going from her. "We will all find ourselves suitable matches with gentlemen to whom we can lose our hearts, knowing that their hearts love us in return."

As her friends smiled, Cassandra's heart began to soar. This Season was going to be an excellent one, she was sure.

Yes, she had her cousin's warnings, but she also had her friends' support in her quest to find a gentleman who would love her; a gentleman she would carry in her heart for all of her days. Surely such a fellow would not be so difficult to find?

CHAPTER TWO

"I should like to hear something... significant... about you this Season."

Jonathan rolled his eyes, knowing precisely what his mother expected. This was now his fourth Season in London and, as yet, he had not found himself a bride – much to his mother's chagrin, of course. On his part, it was quite deliberate and, although he had stated as much to his mother on various occasions, it did not seem to alter her attempts to encourage him toward matrimony.

"You are aware that you did not have to come to London with me, Mother?" Jonathan shrugged his shoulders. "If you had remained at home, then you would not have suffered as much concern, surely?"

"It is a legitimate concern, which I would suffer equally, no matter where I am!" his mother shot back fiercely. "You have not given me any expectation of a forthcoming marriage and I continually wonder and worry over the lack of an heir! You are the Marquess of Sherbourne! You have responsibilities!"

Jonathan scowled.

"Responsibilities I take seriously, Mother. However, I will not be forced into–"

"I have already heard whispers of your various entanglements during last Season. I can hardly imagine that this Season will be any better."

At this, Jonathan took a moment to gather himself, trying to control the fierce surge of anger now burning in his soul. When he spoke, it was with a quietness he could barely keep hold of.

"I assure you, such whispers have been greatly exaggerated. I am not a scoundrel."

He could tell immediately that this did not please his mother, for she shook her head and let out a harsh laugh.

"I do not believe that," she stated, her tone still fierce. "Especially when my *dear* friend, Lady Edmonds, tells me that you were attempting to entice her daughter into your arms!" Her eyes closed tight. "The fact that she is still willing to even be my friend is very generous indeed."

A slight pang of guilt edged into Jonathan's heart, but he ignored it with an easy shrug of his shoulders.

"Do you truly think that Lady Hannah was so unwilling? That I had to coerce her somehow?" Seeing how his mother pressed one hand to her mouth, he rolled his eyes for the second time. "It is the truth I tell you, Mother. Whether you wish to believe me or not, any rumors you have heard have been greatly exaggerated. For example, Lady Hannah was the one who came to seek *me* out, rather than it being me pursuing her."

His mother rose from her chair, her chin lifting and her face a little flushed.

"I will not believe that Lady Hannah, who is so delicate a creature, would even have *dreamt* of doing such a thing as that!"

"You very may very well not believe it, and that would not surprise me, given that everyone else holds much the same opinion." Spreading both hands, Jonathan let out a small sigh. "I may not be eager to wed, Mother, but I certainly am not a scoundrel or a rogue, as you appear to believe me to be."

His mother looked away, her hands planted on her hips, and Jonathan scowled, frustrated by his mother's lack of belief in his character. During last Season, he had been utterly astonished when Lady Hannah had come to speak with him directly, only to attempt to draw him into some sort of assignation. And she only in her first year out in Society as well! Jonathan had always kept far from those young ladies who were newly out – even, as in this case, from those who had been so very obvious in their eagerness. No doubt being a little upset by his lack of willingness, Lady Hannah had gone on to tell her mother a deliberate untruth about him, suggesting that *he* had been the one to try to negotiate something warm between them. And now, it seemed, his own mother believed that same thing. It was not the first time that such rumors had been spread about gentlemen – himself included and, on some occasions, Jonathan admitted, the rumors had come about because of his actions. But other whispers, such as this, were grossly unfair. Yet who would believe the word of a supposedly roguish gentleman over that of a young lady? There was, Jonathan considered, very little point in arguing.

"I will not go near Lady Hannah this Season, if that is what is concerning you." With a slight lift of his shoulders, Jonathan tried to smile at his mother, but only received an angry glare in return. "I assure you that I have no interest in Lady Hannah! She is not someone I would consider even stepping out with, were I given the opportunity." Protesting

204 | ROSE PEARSON

his innocence was futile, he knew, but yet the words kept coming. "I do not even think her overly handsome."

"Are you stating that she is ugly?"

Jonathan closed his eyes, stifling a groan. It seemed that he could say nothing which would bring his mother any satisfaction. The only thing to please her would be if he declared himself betrothed to a suitable young lady. At present, however, he had very little intention of doing anything of the sort. He was quite content with his life, such as it was. The time to continue the family line would come soon enough, but he could give it a few more years until he had to consider it.

"No, mother, Lady Hannah is not ugly." Seeing how her frown lifted just a little, he took his opportunity to escape. "Now, if you would excuse me, I have an afternoon tea to attend." His mother's eyebrows lifted with evident hope, but Jonathan immediately set her straight. "With Lord and Lady Yardley," he added, aware of how quickly her features slumped again. "I have no doubt that you will be a little frustrated by the fact that my ongoing friendship with Lord and Lady Yardley appears to be the most significant connection in my life, but he is a dear friend and his wife has become so also. Surely you can find no complaint there!" His mother sniffed and looked away, and Jonathan, believing now that there was very little he could say to even bring a smile to his mother's face, turned his steps towards the door. "Good afternoon, Mother."

So saying, he strode from the room, fully aware of the heavy weight of expectation that his mother continually placed upon his shoulders. He could not give her what she wanted, and her ongoing criticism was difficult to hear. She did not have proof of his connection to Lady Hannah but, all the same, thought poorly of him. She would criticize his close acquaintance with Lord and Lady Yardley also! His friendships were quickly thrown aside, as were his explanations and his pleadings of innocence - there was nothing he could say or do that would bring her even a hint of satisfaction, and Jonathan had no doubt that, during this Season, he would be a disappointment to her all over again.

"GOOD AFTERNOON, YARDLEY."

His friend beamed at him, turning his head for a moment as he poured two measures of brandy into two separate glasses.

"Sherbourne! Good afternoon, do come in. It appears to be an excellent afternoon, does it not?"

Jonathan did so, his eyes on his friend, gesturing to the brandy on the table.

"It will more than excellent once you hand me the glass which I hope is mine."

Lord Yardley chuckled and obliged him.

"And yet, it seems as though you are troubled all the same," he remarked, as Jonathan took a sip of what he knew to be an excellent French brandy. "Come then, what troubles you this time?" Lifting an eyebrow, he grinned as Jonathan groaned aloud. "I am certain it will have something to do with your dear mother."

Letting out an exasperated breath, Jonathan gesticulated in the air as Lord Yardley took a seat opposite him.

"She wishes me to be just as you are." Jonathan took a small sip of his brandy. "Whereas I am less and less inclined to wed myself to *any* young lady who has her approval... simply because she will have my mother's approval!"

Lord Yardley chuckled and then took a sip from his

glass.

"That is difficult indeed! You are quite right to state that *you* will be the one to decide when you wed... so long as it is not simply because you are avoiding your responsibilities."

"I am keenly aware of my responsibilities, which is precisely *why* I avoid matrimony. I already have a great deal of demands on my time – I can only imagine that to add a wife to that burden would only increase it!"

"You are quite mistaken."

Jonathan chuckled darkly.

"You only say so because your wife is an exceptional lady. I think you one of the *few* gentlemen who finds themselves so blessed."

Lord Yardley shrugged.

"Then I must wonder if you believe the state of matrimony to be a death knell to a gentleman's heart. I can assure you it is quite the opposite."

"You say that only because you have found contentment," Jonathan shot back quickly. "There are many gentlemen who do not find themselves so comfortable."

Lord Yardley shrugged.

"There may be more than you know." He picked up his brandy glass again. "And if that is what you seek from your forthcoming marriage to whichever young lady you choose, then why do you not simply search for a suitable match, rather than doing very little other than entertain yourself throughout the Season? You could find a lady who would bring you a great deal of contentment, I am sure."

Resisting the urge to roll his eyes, Jonathan spread both hands, one still clutching his brandy, the other one empty.

"Because I do not feel the same urgency about the matter as my mother," he stated firmly. "When the time is right, I will find an excellent young lady who will fill my heart with such great affection that I will be unable to do anything but look into her eyes and find myself lost. *Then* I will know that she is the one I ought to wed. However, until that moment comes, I will continue on, just as I am at present." For a moment he thought that his friend would laugh at him, but much to his surprise, Lord Yardley simply nodded in agreement. There was not even a hint of a smile on his lips, but rather a gentle understanding in his eyes which spoke of acceptance of all that Jonathan had said. "Let us talk of something other than my present situation." Throwing back the rest of his brandy, and with a great and contented sigh, Jonathan set the glass back down on the table to his right. "Your other guests have not arrived as yet, I see. Are you hoping for a jovial afternoon?"

"A cheerful afternoon, certainly, although we will not be overwhelmed by too many guests today." Lord Yardley grinned. "It is a little unfortunate that I shall soon have to return to my estate." His smile faded a little. "I do not like the idea of being away from my wife, but there are many improvements taking place at the estate which must be overseen." His lips pulled to one side for a moment. "Besides which, my wife has her cousin to chaperone this Season."

"Her cousin?" Repeating this, Jonathan frowned as his friend nodded. "You did not mention this to me before."

"Did I not?" Lord Yardley replied mildly, waving one hand as though it did not matter. "Yes, my wife is to be chaperoning her cousin for the duration of the Season. The girl's parents are both on the continent, you understand, and given that she would not have much of a coming out otherwise, my wife thought it best to offer."

Jonathan tried to ignore the frustration within him at the fact that his friend would not be present for the Season, choosing instead to nod.

"How very kind of her. And what is the name of this cousin?"

"Lady Cassandra Chilton." Lord Yardley's gaze flew towards the door. "No doubt you will meet her this afternoon. I do not know what is taking them so long but, then again, I have never been a young lady about to make her first appearance in Society."

Jonathan blinked. Clearly this was more than just an afternoon tea. This Lady Cassandra would be present this afternoon so that she might become acquainted with a few of those within society. Why Lord Yardley had not told him about this before, Jonathan did not know – although it was very like his friend to forget about such details.

"Lady Cassandra is being presented this afternoon?"

His friend nodded.

"Yes, as we speak. I did offer to go with them, of course, but was informed she was already nervous enough, and would be quite contented with just my dear wife standing beside her."

Jonathan nodded and was about to make some remark about how difficult a moment it must be for a young lady to be presented to the Queen, only for the door to open and Lady Yardley herself to step inside.

"Ah, Lord Sherbourne. How delighted I am to see you."

With a genuine smile on her face, she waved at him to remain seated rather than attempt to get up to greet her.

"Good afternoon, Lady Yardley. I do hope the presentation went well?"

"Exceptionally well. Cassandra has just gone up to change out of her presentation gown – those gowns which the Queen requires are so outdated and uncomfortable! She will join us shortly."

The lady threw a broad smile in the direction of her

husband, who then rose immediately from his chair to go towards her. Taking her hands, he pressed a kiss to the back of one and then to the back of the other. It was a display of affection usually reserved only for private moments, but Jonathan was well used to such things between Lord and Lady Yardley. In many ways, he found it rather endearing.

"I am sure that Cassandra did very well with you beside her."

Lady Yardley smiled at her husband.

"She has a great deal of strength," she replied, quietly. "I find her quite remarkable. Indeed, I was proud to be there beside her."

"I have only just been hearing about your cousin, Lady Yardley. I do hope to be introduced to her very soon." Shifting in his chair, Jonathan waved his empty glass at Lord Yardley, who laughed but went in search of the brandy regardless. "You are sponsoring her through the Season, I understand."

His gaze now fixed itself on Lady Yardley, aware of that soft smile on her face.

"Yes, I am." Settling herself in her chair, she let out a small sigh as she did so. "I have no doubt that she will be a delight to society. She is young and beautiful and very well-considered, albeit a little naïve."

A slight frown caught Jonathan's forehead.

"Naïve?"

Lady Yardley nodded.

"Yes, just as every young lady new to society has been, and will be for years to come. She is quite certain that she will find herself hopelessly in love with the very best of a gentleman and that he will seek to marry her by the end of the Season."

"Such things do happen, my dear."

Lady Yardley laughed softly at Lord Yardley's remark, reaching across from her chair to grasp her husband's hand.

"I am not saying that they do not, only that my dear cousin thinks that all will be marvelously well for her in society and that the *ton* is a welcoming creature rather than one to be most cautious of. I, however, am much more on my guard. Not every gentleman who seeks her out will be looking to marry her. Not every gentleman who seeks her out will believe in the concept of love."

"Love?" Jonathan snorted, rolling his eyes to himself as both Lord and Lady Yardley turned their attention towards him. Flushing, he shrugged. "I suppose I would count myself as someone who does not believe such a thing to have any importance. I may not even believe in the concept!"

Lady Yardley's eyes opened wide.

"You mean to say that what Lord Yardley and I share is something you do not believe in?"

Blinking rapidly, Jonathan tried to explain, his chest suddenly tight.

"No, it is not that I do not believe it a meaningful connection which can be found between two people such as yourselves. It is that I personally have no interest in it. I have no intention of marrying someone simply because I find myself in love with them. In truth, I do not know if I am even capable of such a feeling."

"I can assure you that you are, whether or not you believe yourself to be."

Lord Yardley muttered his remark rather quietly and Jonathan took in a slow breath, praying that his friend would not start instructing him on the matter of love."

Lady Yardley smiled and gazed at Jonathan for some moments before taking a breath and continuing.

"All the same, I do want my cousin to be cautious, particularly during this evening's ball. I want her to understand that not every gentleman will be as she expects."

"I am sure such gentlemen will make that obvious all by themselves."

This brought a frown to Lady Yardley's features, but a chuckle came from Lord Yardley instead. Jonathan grinned, just as the door opened and a young lady stepped into the room, beckoned by Lady Yardley. A gentle smile softened her delicate features as she glanced around the room, her eyes finally lingering on Jonathan.

"I feel as though I have walked into something most mysterious since everyone stopped talking the moment I entered." One eyebrow arching, she smiled at him. "I do hope that someone will tell me what it is all about!"

Jonathan rose, as was polite, but his lips seemed no longer able to deliver speech. Even his breath seemed to have fixed itself inside his chest as he stared, his mouth ajar, at the beautiful young woman who had just walked in. Her skin was like alabaster, her lips a gentle pink, pulled into a soft smile as blue eyes sparkled back at him. He had nothing to say and everything to say at the very same time. Could this delightful young woman be Lady Yardley's cousin? And if she was, then why was no one introducing him?

"Allow me to introduce you." As though he had read his thoughts, Lord Yardley threw out one hand towards the young woman. "Might I present Lady Cassandra, daughter to the Earl of Holford. And this, Lady Cassandra, is my dear friend, the Marquess of Sherbourne. He is an excellent sort. You need have no fears with him."

Bowing quickly towards the young woman, Jonathan fought to find his breath.

"I certainly would not be so self-aggrandizing as to say

that I was 'an excellent sort', Lady Cassandra." he was somehow unable to draw his gaze away from her, and his heart leaped in his chest when she smiled all the more. "But I shall be the most excellent companion to you, should you require it, just as I am with Lord and Lady Yardley."

There was a breath of silence, and Jonathan cleared his throat, aware that he had just said more to her than he had ever said to any other young lady upon first making their acquaintance. Even Lord Yardley appeared to be a little surprised, for there was a blink, a smile and, after another long pause, the conversation continued. Lady Yardley gestured for her cousin to come and sit beside her, and the young lady obliged. Jonathan finally managed to drag his eyes away to another part of the room, only just becoming aware of how frantically his heart was beating. Everything he had just said to his friend regarding what would occur should he ever meet a young lady who stole his attention in an instant came back to him. Had he meant those words?

Giving himself a slight shake, Jonathan settled back into his chair, lost in thought as conversation flowed around the room. This was nothing more than an instant attraction, the swift kick of desire which would be gone within a few hours. There was nothing of any seriousness in such a swift response, he told himself. He had nothing to concern himself with and thus, he tried to insert himself back into the conversation just as quickly as he could.

Oh, no, Jonathan likes her! Perhaps he will have to change his mind about becoming leg-shackled! Check out the rest of story in the Kindle Store The Heart of a Gentleman

JOIN MY MAILING LIST

Sign up for my newsletter to stay up to date on new releases, contests, giveaways, freebies, and deals!

Free book with signup!

Monthly Facebook Giveaways! Books and Amazon gift cards!
Join me on Facebook: https://www.facebook.com/rosepearsonauthor

Website: www.RosePearsonAuthor.com

Follow me on Goodreads: Author Page